Eliot Woodward

Archaeology or the stone age in America and Europe

Eliot Woodward

Archaeology or the stone age in America and Europe

ISBN/EAN: 9783742839701

Manufactured in Europe, USA, Canada, Australia, Japa

Cover: Foto ©Andreas Hilbeck / pixelio.de

Manufactured and distributed by brebook publishing software
(www.brebook.com)

Eliot Woodward

Archaeology or the stone age in America and Europe

CATALOGUE

ILLUSTRATING THE CHOICEST SPECIMENS

IN

ARCHAEOLOGY,

INCLUDING

AMULETS, BANNER STONES, DISCOIDAL STONES, PIPES, AXES, CELTS, SPEAR HEADS, ARROW POINTS, Etc., Etc.

ALL SELECTED FROM THE FINEST PORTIONS OF THE COLLECTION OF

MR. NORMAN SPANG,

ETNA, PENN.

Mr. Spang has long been known as a leading Archaeologist, and amongst Collectors he has stood second to no man for his accumulations of relics in Stone, Iron, Bronze, Copper and Shell.

THIS COLLECTION WILL BE SOLD BY AUCTION, INCLUDING THE CABINETS,

BY

Messrs. BANGS & CO.,

739 and 741 Broadway, New York,

THURSDAY, FRIDAY AND SATURDAY,

December 27, 28 and 29, 1888,

Goods on Exhibition on days of sale at 10, A. M., and the sale will begin promptly at 2 P. M.

Catalogue by W. Elliot Woodward.

BOSTON:
T. R. MARVIN & SON, NUMISMATIC PRINTERS.
1888.

------◆●◆------

CORRESPONDENTS are requested to send early orders, thus giving me time to enter them in my books before I leave for New York. It is not an uncommon thing for me to have a greater number of orders than there are lots in the catalogue and many often arrive too late. Writing as I do, with difficulty, it is very desirable that those who wish to entrust their orders to me, should send them as early as possible, that they may receive proper attention. Address as below; but late orders may be sent to me at New York, care of the auctioneers.

The coin dealers of New York, Baltimore, Philadelphia and Lancaster, Pa., will also receive and faithfully execute bids that may be placed with them. As many inquiries are sent me asking for catalogues to complete files, I have prepared a printed list of those that can be supplied, neatly priced in ink, to the 105th inclusive, which will be sold at prices named. This list will be sent on application.

After the sale priced copies of this catalogue printed on heavy tinted paper specially for Collectors will be mailed to order for $1.00 each.

W. ELLIOT WOODWARD,

260 Dudley Street, Roxbury.

CATALOGUE.

PREHISTORICS.

THE following lots from 1 to 28 are mostly from New England, principally in Massachusetts from Salem and Lynn. New England prehistorics are exceedingly rare, the finds having been nearly all exhausted.

1 Large triangular Spear head, narrow stemmed. A fine implement. $4\frac{1}{2}$ x $2\frac{1}{2}$.

2 Spear head, shorter, and not so broad, variegated, of light and dark stone. 5 x 2.

3 Spear head, large, nearly black. 5 x $2\frac{1}{2}$.

4 Spear head of good form; fine. 6 x $1\frac{1}{2}$.

5 Spear head, large, rough. 4 x $1\frac{1}{2}$.

6 Spear head, nearly black. $3\frac{1}{2}$ x $1\frac{1}{2}$.

7 Spear head, same material. 3 x 1.

8 Spear head, broad, bifurcated base, notched; of white stone, fine. $3\frac{1}{4}$ x $1\frac{1}{4}$.

9 Spear head, same form. 4 x $1\frac{1}{2}$.

10 Spear head, sides nearly parallel; fine. $4\frac{1}{2}$ x $1\frac{1}{4}$.

11 Great Spear head, base broken, nearly ovate, white or flesh colored. 4 x $2\frac{1}{4}$.

12 Spear head, base rounded and smooth; large size. 4 x 1.

13 Spear head, sides deeply notched, of dark color. $3\frac{3}{4}$ x $1\frac{1}{4}$.

14 Spear head, broad base; fine. 4 x $1\frac{1}{4}$.

15 Spear point, bevelled and deeply notched, of American flint; from Essex Co., Mass. 3 x 2.

16 Bevelled Spear point, of reddish flesh color. $2\frac{1}{2}$ x $1\frac{1}{4}$.

17 Bevelled rotary Spear point, of dark American flint; Essex Co., Mass. 3 x 1½.

18 Notched Spear point of chert, Essex Co., Mass. 2½ x 1½.

19 Hollow base Spear point, barb broken. 2½ x 1½.

20 Spear points, deeply barbed, of different colored flint; large size. 3 pcs.

21 Arrow points, rather below the average size, some barbed, some triangular; a variety, rude but fine; mostly from Essex Co., Mass. 48 pcs.

22 Spear heads of large size and rude workmanship. 10 pcs.

23 Spear points and Arrow heads; from Essex Co., Mass. 14 pcs.

24 Large and small spear heads and Arrow points; barbed, triangular, and various forms; a variety.

25 A similar lot, large and small, some Fish spears once used for catching suckers, and used for the same purpose now.

26 Spear heads and Arrow points; some are translucent and almost transparent; various sizes and quality of material. 26 pcs.

27 Spear points and Arrow heads, one is almost like a semi-lunar Scandinavian knife, several are drills or borers; a fine assortment. 46 pcs.

28 Arrow points from Kyle's Mound, Ky., and Meigs Co., Ohio; a variety, mostly small, all marked. 12 pcs.

29 A similar variety from Mason Co., W. Va. 16 pcs.

30 Minute Arrow points from Oregon. 11 pcs.

31 Oval Sinker of granite, grooved longitudinally; fine and a scarce form. 5 x 3.

32 Similar, but in form less pronounced. 4 x 3.

33 Tomahawk, or grooved axe, double headed; Princeton, Mass. 4½ x 3½.

34 Plumb-bob, oval, of dark color, with knobs at both ends; Ipswich, Mass. 3 x 1½.

35 Plumb-bob of dark color, elongated oval; Abington, Mass. 3 x 2.

36 Plumb-bob, with knob at the end; Chelmsford, N. H. 2½ x 1¾.

37 Discoidal double concave; from Ky. 2½ x 1.

38 Very large Spear head ; slate, rude ; Marblehead, Mass. : rare form and size. 8 x 3½.

39 Large Spear head of slate ; Kentucky. 5½ x 3.

40 Spear head, large, elliptical, of dark slate ; Ontario, Can. 6½ x 2½.

41 Large rude implement, or Knife ; Nahant, Mass. 4½ x 3½.

42 Semi-lunar Scraper, slate ; Marblehead, Mass. 4 x 2.

43 Rude Knife, slate. 4 x 2.

44 Discs of slate, various sizes, each about 3 in. dia. 4 pcs.

45 Phallic-shaped implement, the head resembles a bear ; Chelsea, Mass. 7 x 1½.

46 Semi-globular objects ; Mass. 7 pcs.

47 Banner stone, blocked out, not finished ; two other fragments, hammer stone, etc. 6 pcs.

48 Amulet or saddle-stone, of metamorphic slate, from New England ; this object when found in New England is of the most extreme rarity. 4½ x 1½.

49 Banner stone, triangular in form, with large perforation ; of metamorphic slate ; rare ; Ontaria, Canada. 3¾ x 2½.

50 Banner stone, semi-lunar, one end repaired ; No. Amherst, Mass. 5 x 1½.

51 Amulet, head with large eyes ; very rare, and of rare form ; Canton, Mass. 1½ x 1.

52 Pendant, both sides nearly covered with tally marks ; red slate, perforated. 3 x 1½.

53 Pendant, oval, small perforation, dark slate ; Ipswich, Mass. 3 x 1½.

54 Pendants, perforated ; broken. 2 pcs.

55 Pipe, of slate, with square bowl ; fine and rare ; from the ancient grave find, excavated by Mr. Vicary, Chelsea, Mass. 6 x 2½.

56 Pipe of the Mound builders' pattern, slate ; fine, and very rare. 2 x 1½.

57 Pipe of catlinite, inlaid with lead ; modern Indian, but still very fine and rare. 5 x 3.

58 Pipe of catlinite ; round, artistic, very fine and rare. 5½ x 3.

59 Pipe of modern Indian workmanship ; undoubtedly the work of Cherokees ; a fine specimen of Indian carving. 2½ x 1½.

60 Pipe, slate, covered with two ferules of copper ; Chelsea, Mass. $2\frac{1}{2}$ x $\frac{3}{4}$.

61 Hollow Gouge with deep short depression ; very fine and rare indeed ; Rowley, Mass. $6\frac{1}{2}$ x 1.

62 Hollow Gouge, the depression much elongated ; a very fine and rare implement ; Reading, Mass. $9\frac{1}{2}$ x 2.

63 Gouge, deeply grooved ; very fine, appears to be reddish jasper. 5 x 2.

64 Gouge of fine form, of bluish colored slate ; the reverse has a longitudinal groove. $8\frac{1}{2}$ x 2.

65 Gouge of red stone ; fine and rare ; the reverse has a transverse groove for the purpose of fastening it to a handle ; Princeton, Mass. 5 x $1\frac{1}{2}$.

66 Flattened Gouge, broad. 6 x 2.

67 Gouge, nearly adze-form, with transverse depression on the back side ; fine and scarce. 6 x 2.

68 Gouge, adze-form ; a rare implement, but its appearance is rude. 6 x $2\frac{1}{2}$.

69 Celt, of granite, unusually graceful form ; near Springfield, Mass. 6 x $1\frac{1}{2}$.

70 Celt of dense and hard greenish stone, polished ; rare ; Denmark. 4 x 1.

71 Celt of polished stone ; Princeton, Mass. $4\frac{1}{2}$ x 2.

72 Celt of feldspar, shaped like a shoe horn ; Florida. $4\frac{1}{2}$ x 2.

72a Celt, similar to the last ; same location. 3 x $1\frac{1}{2}$.

73 Thick Celt of granite ; Nahant, Mass. 4 x $1\frac{1}{2}$.

74 Sandstone Celt ; fine ; Marblehead, Mass, $3\frac{1}{2}$ x $1\frac{1}{2}$.

75 Thick, broad Celt ; Rocky pasture, Lynn, Mass. 3 x 2.

76 Discoidal Stone. thin, double convex ; Kentucky. 3 in. dia.

77 Stone Bead. $\frac{3}{4}$ in. dia.

78 Scraper, with rounded edge ; fine and rare ; Turner's Falls, Mass. 3 x 2.

79 Knife of flint, from Denmark ; fine. $4\frac{1}{2}$ x 1.

80 Drills or perforators ; So. Carolina and Pa. ; very fine : from $1\frac{1}{2}$ to 3 in. in length. 4 pcs.

81 Base of prehistoric Pipe ; Marblehead, Mass. $1\frac{1}{2}$ x 1.

82 Slate Needle for sewing reindeer skins. $7\frac{1}{2}$ x $\frac{1}{2}$.

83 Stone carving from Vancouver's Island. 3 x 1.

84 Needles. etc., of bone, for sewing reindeer skins.

85 Rude Celts. large and small. 7 pcs.

86 Polished Celt, resembles jade ; Peabody, Mass. 1¾ x 1½.

87 Triangular Plumb-bob and other objects, one of polished red stone. 4 pcs.

88 Copper implement, or celt, found at Chelsea, Mass., by Mr. Vicary : very rare. 2½ x 1¼.

89 Disc of brass or copper, also found in the ancient grave at Chelsea. 1¼ in. dia.

90 Flint Dagger, with carved handle beautifully wrought ; one of the finest daggers 1 have ever seen : Scandinavia. 7½ x 2.

91 Another flint Dagger from Scandinavia, finely chipped or carved ; rare. 7½ x 1½.

92 Another chipped Dagger from the same locality ; a beautiful object. 6½ x 1½.

PENDANTS AND GORGETS.

The following Prehistoric relics which are usually classed as Pendants, Gorgets and Banner stones, are particularly fine and of exceptional beauty and rarity. A large portion of them are polished and of beautiful material, comprising hematite, jasper and various slates, etc., etc.

The owner of these objects, recently purchased from Mr. Norman Spang, of Etna, Pa., believes that a finer collection is unknown, and for beauty and extent it is believed to be unique.

Pendants mostly with two holes and of forms as distinguished and described.

93 Pendant, square oblong, two holes; of metamorphic slate. very handsome : Huron Co., Ohio. 4 x 2½.

94 Gorget of veined and clouded slate, quadrangular, two partly finished perforations ; Miami Co., Ohio. 4 x 2.

95 Gorget, same form and material as the last ; Darke Co., Ohio. 3¼ x 1¾.

96 Slate Scraper of unique form, end rounded and semilunar. double perforations ; E. Tenn. 4 x 3.

97 Pendant. sides contracted, of dark purple slate ; two small perforations ; Huron Co., Ohio. 5 x 2½.

98 Oval Gorget of hematite, two perforations, from Lincoln Co., Tenn. ; rare. 3¼ x 2¼.

99   Oval Gorget of hematite, resembles the last; Barton
     Co., Alabama; rare. 4 x 2.

100 Gorget, in form, style and workmanship resembles the
     last, two minute holes; Oneida Co., N. Y. $3\frac{1}{2}$ x 2.

101 Gorget, oval, handsome metamorphic slate, polished;
     two small perforations; Shelby Co., Ohio. 6 x $2\frac{1}{2}$.

102 Gorget, two small perforations, sides contracted narrow-
     er than the ends; of dark purple slate; Warren,
     Ohio. $3\frac{1}{4}$ x $1\frac{3}{4}$.

103 Gorget, coffin-shaped, of steatite; Grommett Co., Ga.
     4 x $1\frac{1}{2}$.

104 Elliptical Gorget, metamorphic slate, appears to have
     been blocked out for an amulet with considerable
     care. $4\frac{1}{2}$ x 2.

105 Gorget, sides nearly parallel, dark slate; from a mound
     on Beaver River, Rochester, Beaver Co., Pa. $4\frac{1}{2}$ x $1\frac{1}{4}$.

106 Gorget, imperfect, from Crawford's Cave, Bull Run,
     Knox County, Tenn.; found with stalactites, pot, etc.
     2 x $1\frac{1}{2}$.

107 Gorget, used as a whetstone by the Indians; Fairfield.
     Co., S. C. 3 x $1\frac{1}{2}$.

108 Gorget, used as a bullet mould amongst the ancient
     Indians; South Western N. C. $2\frac{1}{2}$ x $1\frac{1}{4}$.

109 Gorget, two perforations, metamorphic slate; Ohio. 2
     x $1\frac{1}{2}$.

110 Gorget, four perforations; Seneca Co., Ohio. 2 x 2.

111 Gorget of steatite; Western Pa. 3 x $1\frac{1}{2}$.

112 Canoe-shaped Gorget, two small perforations; S. West-
     ern N. C. 4 x 2.

113 Drilled object, two perforations; Lodi, Miss. 1 x 1.

114 Gorget, long, and sides nearly parallel, greenish slate;
     Rhea Co., E. Tenn. 5 x $1\frac{1}{4}$.

115 Gorget of soapstone, edges corrugated; Lincoln Co.,
     Tenn. $2\frac{1}{4}$ x 1.

116 Gorget, ends nearly pointed, large perforations; San-
     dusky River, Wyandott Co., Ohio. 6 x $1\frac{3}{4}$.

117 Gorget, elliptical shaped, has no perforations; Green
     Co., Tenn. 5 x 2.

118 Gorget of hematite or red slate, drilled but incomplete;
     near Lodi, Montgomery Co., Miss. $2\frac{3}{4}$.

119 Gorget, two very large perforations, of somewhat coni-
     cal elliptical form; Rabun Co., Ga. 3 x 1.

20 Gorget, three perforations, brown slate and broken off; Seneca Co., Ohio. 2½ x 1½.

21 Gorget, elliptical, two perforations, small; Clay Co., N. C. 31½ x 1½.

22 Gorget, elliptical, somewhat canoe-shaped; Cherokee Co., N. C. 4½ x 1¼.

23 Pendant or scraper, in form somewhat like No. 96. Dark slate; Little Pigeon Mound, E. Tenn. A fine and rare object, slightly imperfect. 6 x 5.

24 Slate Pendant, polished, a rare form; Allen Co., Ohio. 5 x 2½.

25 Pendant, sides contracted, one large perforation; Huron Co., Ohio. 4 x 2.

26 Pendant, ends expanded, one large hole; Cumberland River, Ky. 4¼ x 1¾.

27 Pendant, one hole near the end; Clay Co., Ky. 3¾ x 1¼.

28 Pendant, plumb-bob shape. 3¼ x 1¼.

29 Pendant, large perforation; Huron Co., Ohio. 3½ x 1½.

30 Pendant, sides expanded; Hog Island, Beaver Co., Ohio. 4½ x 1¾.

31 Pendant, approaching elliptical in form; Shelby Co., Ohio. 2¾ x 1½.

32 Pendant, metamorphic slate, top expanded; fine specimen. 4½ x 1½.

33 Pendant, or ornament of ribbon slate; Logan Co., Ohio. 3¼ x 2.

34 Pendant of metamorphic slate, pentagonal, very fine; Western Iowa. 4¾ x 2¾.

35 Pendant, one large drilled perforation, handsome red color; Chariton Co., Mo. 4 x 2.

36 Pendant, broken across the middle; Seneca Co., Ohio. 1½ x 1.

37 Pendant, large perfortion near the middle, marks by disintegration of age; Seneca Co., Ohio. 4½ x 2.

38 Pendant, has been split; from Natural Bridge, near Creelsboro, Russell Co., Ky. 2¼ x 1.

39 Pendant, curved, semi-elliptical; Breckenridge Co., Ky. 3½ x 1.

40 Pendant, red jasper; Franklin Co., Mo. 4 x 1¾.

141   Pendant, red ribbon jasper, polished, one end expanded ; Clay Co., Ky. 3 x 1½.

142   Pendant, narrowed at the sides ; found near Jones Cove, Sevier Co., Tenn. 4 x 1¾.

143   Pendant, large perforation ; Warren, Ohio. 3 x 1½.

144   Pendant, curved, one end broken ; Breckenridge Co., Ky. 3¼ x 1½.

145   Pendant, sides expanded ; Branch Co., Mich. 3¾ x 2.

146   Pendant, small perforation near the end ; Swaine Co., S. West N. C. 4 x 1.

147   Pendants, two broken ; from Florida, Kentucky, and Tenn. 3 pcs.

148   Pendant, nearly square, of slatestone ; Vigo Co., Ind. 4 x ½.

149   Pendant, probably a modern ornament of slate, made by the Cherokee Indians ; Cherokee Co., N. C. 3 x 2.

150   Fine polished implement of red or purple slate ; sides and ends contracted ; James Co., Tenn. 5 x 4.

151   Another fine implement, in form and color resembling the last ; near Greenwich, Huron Co., Ohio. 3¾ x 2.

152   Gorget, has two finished perforations, thick in the middle ; Shelby Co., Ohio. 3 x 2.

153   Amulet shaped Gorget, sides contracted, edges nearly parallel, green slate ; Huron Co., Ohio. 4 x 1¼.

154   Gorget, elliptical, with ends truncated, green slate, fine ; Huron Co., Ohio. 4 x 1½.

155   Slate Gorget, imperforate, one end narrowed ; Meigs Co., Tenn. 4 x 1½.

156   Slate Gorget, contracted at the ends, finely finished ; James Co., Tenn. 4 x 1.

157   Gorget, surface marked with incised lines, green slate, Seneca Co., Ohio. 4 x 2.

158   Gorget, imperforate, oval, of dark slate, polished ; Oregon. 3 x 2.

159   Slate Gorgets, one transversely broken ; E. Va., and Arkansas. 2 pcs.

BANNER STONES.

160   Banner stone, of ribbon or metamorphic slate, shaped like a cocked hat, very large perforation ; extra fine and well made ; Holmes Co., Ohio. 4½ x 2⅞.

161 Banner stone, metamorphic slate, handsomely made, with small unfinished perforation; Williams Co., Ohio. 5½ x 2½.

162 Banner stone with deep notches at the sides, of polished ribbon slate, a very unusual form; Williams Co., Ohio. 4½ x 3.

163 Banner stone, green slate, small perforation, butterfly shape; Woods Co., Ohio. 5½ x 2½.

164 Banner stone, of hard material, approaches the cocked hat in form, somewhat like 160; large fine transverse perforation; Habersham Co., Ga. 4 x 2.

165 Banner stone of red Jasper or slate, a very fine implement and of singular form; Shelby Co., Ohio. 4½ x 2.

166 Banner stone of ribbon or metamorphic slate, polished; fine and rare. De Kalb Co., Ind. 4 x 1½.

167 Banner stone, shaped like a pair of curved horns, dark slate; Shelby Co., Ohio. 5½ x 1¼.

168 Banner stone, butterfly shape, elliptical in form; Union Co., Ohio. 5 x 2.

169 Banner stone of ribbon slate, formed like a pair of horns polished and very fine; Bear Creek, Fulton Co., Ohio. 3½ x 1.

170 Banner stone of ribbon slate, handsomely polished, similar to last in form; Shelby Co., Ohio. 3½ x 1¼.

171 Banner stone, shaped like a pair of horns, with the ends enlarged; Licking Co., Ohio. 3½ x 1.

172 Banner stone, in form like a two-bladed axe, polished, fine; Wood Co., Ohio. 3½ x 1½.

173 Two-horn-shaped Banner stone, metamorphic slate, large perforation; Shelby Co., Ohio. 4 x 1.

174 Two-horn-shaped Banner stone, one end truncated, dark shot-colored stone; Chattooga River, Rabun Co., Ga. 4 x 1½.

175 Banner stone, in shape a double-bladed pick-axe, slate, fine; Shelby Co., Ohio. 5 x 1.

176 Banner stone of ribbon slate, a pair of horns base to base, a large perforation with deep notch where the base joins; Carter Co., Tenn, 3¾ x 1.

177 Banner stone of strange form, slate, has deeply grooved perforation, ribbed from end to end; Huron Co., Ohio. 3 x 2½.

TUBES, ETC.

178 Tube of indurated clay. Concerning this tube Mr. Spang remarks:— " The only specimen of this material I have ever possessed." Beautifully polished inside and out. They are of the same class as those found in the old burial ground at Swanton, Vt., described in my catalogue No. 92; at present these tubes are sometimes classed as pipes ; Wyandotte Co., Ohio. $3\frac{1}{2}$ x1.

179 Smoking Tube of indurated clay, very fine, but not so perfect as the last; imperfect through a longitudinal fracture ; Ohio. $4\frac{1}{2}$ x 1.

180 Slate Tube, finely made ; Barton, Ala. $2\frac{1}{4}$ x 1.

181 Tube with large perforation, of ribbon slate, polished, fine ; Muskingum Co., Ohio. 4 x $1\frac{3}{4}$.

182 Tube of red breccia, fine and rare material ; Breckenridge Co., Ky. $2\frac{1}{2}$ x $2\frac{1}{2}$.

183 Tube or banner stone, ribbed on both sides over a large perforation ; Sevier Co., E. Tenn. 3 x 2.

184 Fine Tube of polished slate, ribbed on both sides over a large perforation ; Bear Creek, Williams Co., Ohio. 3x $1\frac{1}{2}$.

185 Polished Tube of ribbon slate, handsomely marked ; surface find, Huron Co., Ohio. 3 x 1.

186 Fine Tube with unusually large perforation ; Polk Co., Tenn. 3 $1\frac{1}{2}$.

187 Flattened Tube, thick, with large perforation; Clay Co., N. C. $2\frac{1}{2}$ x $1\frac{1}{2}$.

188 Tube, side with large groove, large perforation ; Mt. Pleasant, Fayette Co., Pa. $2\frac{1}{2}$ x 1.

189 Tube, apparently of Mound pottery ; the surface has a screw-form thread ; Ky. $1\frac{1}{4}$ x $\frac{3}{4}$.

190 Pipe, or perforated stone, polished surface ; Clay Co., N. C. $1\frac{3}{4}$ x $1\frac{1}{2}$.

191 Tube of fine ribbon slate, polished ; Hudson Co., Ohio. 2 x $1\frac{1}{2}$.

192 Tube of equally fine ribbon slate, large perforation ; Ky. 2 x 2.

193 Tube of ribbon slate, nearly ball-shape ; Williams Co., Ohio. 2 x $1\frac{1}{2}$.

194 Tube, flattened, of colors variegated, a rare material; Polk Co., E. Tenn. 2½ x 2.
195 Tube, in form a double-headed axe, ribbon slate; Licking Co., Ohio. 2 x 1½.
196 Tube, in shape a small tomahawk, of ribbon slate; Huron Co., Ohio. 2 x 1.
197 Another tomahawk Tube, very similar to the last, green slate ; Clay Co., N. C. 1½ x 1.
198 Small Tube of ribbon slate, large perforation ; Logan Co., Ohio. 1½ x 1.

PIPES.

199 Calumet, or pipe of peace, of duck shape, and nearly natural size, and some imitation of plumage, of green stone, a very rare pipe ; found in Chattahooche River, Gwinnett Co., N. C. 9 x 5½.
200 Council Pipe, duck shape, of reddish stone ; fine and of extreme rarity. Macon Co., N. C. 9½ x 5.
201 Parrot or duck Pipe of mica slate ; it bears some resemblance on its surface to plumage ; taken from a mound in Barton Co., Ga. ; a fine and remarkable pipe. 8 x 4.
202 Large Calumet or peace pipe, of steatite, ornamented with several incised lines ; Rabun Co., Ga. 5 x 3.
203 Another Calumet of large size and similar work to the last ; Chattooga River, Rabun Co., Ga. 6½ x 4.
204 Calumet, of red mica slate, a fine and rare pipe ; Swaine Co., N. C. 4½ x 4.
205 Calumet, of canoe-shape, a strange unique form ; sandstone, finely wrought ; near Cane Creek, Towns Co., North Ga. 7 x 2½.
206 Calumet, of rude though not ungraceful form, sandstone or perhaps indurated clay; Blue Ridge, Fannin Co., Ga. 5 x 3.
207 Pipe ; looks like the head of an animal, sandstone. rare and fine ; found in an Indian grave near Old Town, Va. 4 x 8.
208 Frog Pipe of sandstone ; an unique form ; Durkee Co., Ohio. 4 x 3.
209 Turtle Pipe, sandstone, very curious ; Logan Co., Ohio. 4½ x 4.

210 Large Pipe, mica slate, somewhat broken; Sevier Co., Tenn. $3\frac{1}{2}$ x $3\frac{1}{2}$.

211 Large Pipe, slate with ribbon markings; Tishomingo Co., Miss. 4 x 2.

212 Mound builders' Pipe, of pottery; from a mound on Deer Island, opposite Biloxi, Miss. 4 x 3.

213 Another Mound builders' Pipe, of pottery; Jefferson Co., Ark. 3 x 2.

214 Mound builders' pottery pipe, marked with ancient lines; E. Tenn. $5\frac{1}{2}$ x 4.

215 Mound builders' pottery Pipe, stem marked in light colors, a portion white; E. Tenn. $4\frac{1}{2}$ x $1\frac{3}{4}$.

216 Prehistoric Pipe, in material resembling marble, head serpent form; Frazier Mound, E. Tenn. $2\frac{1}{2}$ x $1\frac{1}{2}$.

217 Double-headed image Pipe, believed to be of the Mound builders', from nature; a most remarkable pipe, found on the farm of Judge Breckenridge, near Natrona, Allegheny, Pa. $2\frac{1}{2}$ x $1\frac{1}{2}$.

218 Pipe of Mound builders' pottery, bold, much elongated, rare; E. Tenn. $2\frac{1}{4}$ x 1.

219 Pipe, marble, with two perforations; found in a small grave, on a mound in Pigeon River, Tenn. $2\frac{1}{2}$ x $1\frac{1}{4}$.

220 Ancient Pipe, believed not to be prehistoric, but thought to be of English workmanship; Jefferson Co. $4\frac{1}{2}$ x 2.

221 Prehistoric Pipe, figure presumed to be an Indian or Mound builder; notice the peculiarity of the eyes and mouth, which are believed to be unusual; Durkee Co., Ohio. 2 x $1\frac{1}{2}$.

222 Small size prehistoric Pipe, thought to be Mound builders'; Clay Co., N. C. $1\frac{1}{2}$ x 1.

223 Mound builders' Pipe, of pottery, monitor shape; Allegheny Co., Pa. $2\frac{1}{2}$ x 2.

224 Mound builders' Pipe, of pottery, foot-shaped; Mandeville Co., Miss. 3 x 2.

225 Ancient Pipe, Mound builders', with the head of a bear, or perhaps of a reptile, the mouth open and broad; a rare and curious pipe; Lewis Co., Ky. $3\frac{1}{2}$ x 2.

226 Pipe of calcite; Shelby Co., Ohio. $2\frac{1}{2}$ x $1\frac{1}{2}$.

227 Ancient Pipe in shape of a small animal with horns, polished; Tarentum, Allegheny Co., Pa. 2 x $1\frac{1}{2}$.

228 Pipe, much smoked " in the antiquity," the face covered with deep incised lines ; a fine and curious old pipe ; L'Anse, Mich. 2 x 1½.

229 Banner stone, pipe-shape, somewhat like a pair of horns ; from Frazier Mound, Knox Co., Tenn. 3 x 1½.

230 Pipe of ribbon slate, fine and a rare form ; Shelby Co., Ohio. 2½ x 1.

2.75 231 Ancient Pipe, the front ornamented with a carving which is unmistakably Indian or prehistoric; Oneida, N. Y. 3½ x 2.

232 Mound builders' Pipe of pottery and very ancient ; Polk Co., Tenn. 2½ x 1½.

233 Mound builders' Pipe of mica slate, ancient ; Barton, Alabama. 3 x 2.

234 Mound builders' Pipe ; on one side there appears to have been a figure in bas relief ; Cooper Co., Mo. 3 x 2.

235 Pipe of Mound builders' pottery, surface covered with deep incised lines ; said by the collector to be very common in California, but that this is the only specimen he has ever seen from the Valley of the Mississippi. 4½ x 1½.

236 Stone Tube or pipe ; Mr. Spang says of this :— " The only object of this kind and form that I have ever owned." A rarity from Washington Co., Ohio. 4½ x 1½.

237 Snake-head Pipe ; the snake appears in the act of swallowing the bowl ; curious and rare; found beside the big mound, Franklin, N. C. 2½ x 1.

238 Stone Pipe from Jefferson Co., N. Y. ; ancient. 2½ x 1.

239 Pipe of granite, one of the most ancient in the collection ; Georgia. 3 x 2.

240 Ancient Pipe of Mound builders' pottery ; from a mound in La Porte Co., Indiana. 2½ x 1.

241 Mound builders' Pipe of the characteristic form in which this object is usually found ; Oneida Co., N. Y. 3 x 1½.

242 Pipe, doubtless from the Mound builders ; made of a bog iron ore concretion ; near Tulip, Dallas Co., Ark. 2 x 1½.

243 Pipe of stone, marked with lines and deep incised figures ; appears to be and doubtless is of Mound builders' origin ; Hillsdale Co., Ohio. 3 x 2½.

244 Pipe of calcite ; E. Tenn. 2 x 1.

245 Stone Pipe, celt-shaped ; McKee's Rock, Allegheny Co., Pa. 3 x 1½.

246 Mound builders' Pipe of stone ; Cooper Co., Mo. 4 x 2.

247 Pipe of sandstone. 2½ x 1½.

248 Small pottery Pipe, ancient ; found near Wayland, Clark Co., Miss. 2 x 1.

249 Mound builders' Pipe of pottery, with the usual large bowl and contracted stem ; Oneida Co., N. Y. 3½ x 1.

250 Mound Pipe, marked by the same characteristics as the last ; Miami Co., Ohio. 2 x 1.

251 Long graceful Mound builders' Pipe ; from Oneida Co., N. Y. Has been broken but mended. 7 x 1¼.

252 Mound builders' Pipe of pottery, broad, flaring bowl ; the bowl has several fractures, but neatly mended ; E. Tenn. 2 x 2.

253 Mound builders' Pipe, made of pottery or sandstone ; from Vigo Co., Indiana. 2½ x 2.

254 Animal's head Pipe ; from the Mound builders, N. Ga. 2 x 1½.

255 Ancient Pipe-stem or tube ; from Tenn. 3 x 1.

256 Ancient Pipe of stone or pottery ; from Madison Co., N. Y. 3 x 1.

257 A portion of an hour-glass Pipe, of Mound pottery ; Macon Co., Ga. 3½ x 2.

258 Pottery Pipe from Deer Island, near Biloxi, Miss. 1½ x 1.

259 Pipe-stem or tube, of stone ; Rabun Co., Ga. 3½ x 1.

260 Ancient Pipe of ribbon slate, beautifully marked ; from a mound near Franklin River, Porter Co., Ind. 3¼ x ¾.

261 Old Pipe, probably of modern Cherokee manufacture ; represents a hand clasping a bowl, brown mica slate, artistic, fine and rare. Cullusaya, N. C. 3 x 2.

262 Catlinite Pipe, bears a neatly carved cross on side, fine, scarce ; Calhoun Co., Ill. 3 x 1.

C /30 263 Human-faced Pipe ; bears an Indian head, back to the smoker ; very fine ; Clay Co., N. C. 3 x 2.

264 Ancient Pipe, a natural formation evidently geodic ; resembles an ear of corn, and contains a natural crystal projecting inward ; Massac Co., Ill. 2 x 1½.

PIPES OF MODERN CHEROKEE WORKMANSHIP.

265 Pipe of stone, resembling cast iron, fine ; Cherokee Co.,
   N. C. 4 x 1½.

266 Pipe, with figure of a dog seated on the stem, slate, fine ;
   Cherokee Co., N. C. 3 x 2.

267 Pipe of same material, characteristic carving of the
   modern Cherokees : Jackson Co., N. C. 3 x 1¾.

268 Pipe stem and bowl, hexagonal ; elaborately wrought ;
   fine ; Cherokee Co., N. C. 4 x 2.

269 Tobacco-pipe, dark stone, with angular stem, fine ;
   Cherokee Co., N. C. 3½ x 2.

270 Stone Pipe, ancient, resembles a meerschaum both in
   shape and color ; Hawkins Co., Tenn. 4½ x 1½.

271 Cherokee Indian Pipe, has carvings of a squirrel and
   rabbit, both facing the smoker ; Cherokee Co., N. C.
   3 x 1½.

272 Small Pipe or stem, of slate, ancient ; from Rabun Co.,
   Ga. 2½ x ½. Another of the same material. 2 x ½.
   2 pcs.

273 Stone Pipe marked with an arrow and some figures,
   resembles a cigar-holder ; Clay Co., N. C. 2½ x 1.

274 Bowl of an ancient pipe ; appears to be of slate ; Clay
   Co., N. C. 1 x ¾.

275 Red catlinite Pipe, polished ; Wisconsin. 2½ x 2.

276 Catlinite red stone Pipe, carved in shape of a horse.
   polished, ancient; Yellow Medicine, Minn. 4 x 1¼.

277 Ancient Pipe of graceful form, small, of slate. 1½ x ½.

278 Small stone Pipe, of good form ; Clay Co., N. C. 2 x 1.

279 Old Cherokee Pipe, artistic and rare; Cherokee Co.,
   N. C. 3 x 2½.

280 Ancient Pipe, carved from ribbon slate, fine ; Miami
   Co , Ohio. 1½ x 1.

281 Ancient Pipe of rare form, modelled from the leg of a
   woman, handsome and rare ; Hiawassee River, E.
   Tenn. 5 x 1.

282 Red catlinite Pipe ; from Frazier Mound, E. Tenn.
   2 x 1.

283 Stone Pipe, shaped somewhat like a horse's hoof ; No.
   Carolina. 1½ x 1½.

284   Catlinite Pipe stem, fine ; from a mound on Little Pigeon River, E. Tenn. 3 x ¾.

285   Ancient Pipe, in form of a cigar holder ; Clay Co., N. C. 2 x ¾.

286   Stem of an ancient catlinite Pipe, polished, fine ; Cooper Co., Mo. 2 x 1.

287   Ancient Pipe ploughed up on a mound ; Cherokee Co., N. C. 1 x ¾.

288   Tube or pipe stem ; Clay Co., N. C. 3 x ½.

289   Pipe stem or tube ; Clay Co., N. C. 2 x ½.

290   Small stone Pipe ; very fine ; Clay Co., N. C.   1½ x 1.

291   Another small ancient stone Pipe ; same locality as the last. 1½ x 1.

292   Another small ancient stone Pipe. These Pipes are supposed to have been carried by the Indians when on the march ; Cherokee Co., N. C. 1 x 1.

293   Small stone Pipe ; same locality as No. 292. 2 x 1.

294   Several small Pipes, evidently made and carried with like intent ; different localities, all marked. 6 pcs.

295   Small stone Pipe, very fine and rare ; found near Franklin, Macon Co., N. C. 1½ x 1.

OBJECTS IN HEMATITE.

On account of its density, and the exquisite polish of which it allows, hematite was always a favorite object with the prehistoric artificer. Amongst these articles a finer one than No. 296 is seldom if ever obtained.

296   Grooved Axe of brown hematite, polished, extremely large and fine, weight 8¼ lbs., nearly that of steel ; Franklin Co., Mo. Size 6 x 3½.

297   Another grooved hematite Axe of dark brown color ; from Franklin Co,, Mo. 4½ x 3½.

298   Another grooved Axe of brown hematite ; near Potosi, Miss. 4 x 3.

299   Grooved Axe of brown hematite, slightly curved, and fine ; near Potosi, Missouri. 3¾ x 2¾.

300   Grooved Axe of hematite, head broken ; as a fragment extremely fine ; Cooper Co., Mo. 2½ x 2.

301   Celt of polished brown hematite ; one of the very finest I have ever seen ; Quincy, Logan Co., Ohio. 3¼ x 1¾.

302 Celt of polished brown hematite; Butler Co., Pa. $2\frac{1}{2}$ x $1\frac{1}{2}$.

303 Handsome Celt of polished brown hematite. $2\frac{1}{2}$ x $1\frac{1}{2}$.

304 Celt of brown hematite, fine; Missouri. $2\frac{1}{4}$ x $1\frac{3}{4}$.

305 Small Celt of brown hematite, polished; Cooper Co., Mo. $1\frac{1}{2}$ x 1.

306 Celt, red hematite, partly polished; Mason Co., W. Va. 2 x 1.

307 Small polished Celt, of hematite; Missouri. 2 x $\frac{3}{4}$.

308 Small polished Celt of hematite; Mason Co., Va. 1 x 1.

309 Celt or rubbing stone, hematite, used for pigments; Clay Co., N. C. 1 x 1.

310 Tabular red hematite, one side polished; Missouri. $1\frac{1}{2}$ x $1\frac{1}{2}$.

311 Fragments and other specimens of red hematite, all fine; from Missouri. 3 pcs.

312 Small pieces of red hematite, finer than No. 311; from N. C. and Missouri.

312a Truncated cone of red hematite, polished, and of dark liver color; Mammal, so called by Mr. Linney, for a fancy preference on the part of savage man, very fine, scarce; Scioto Township, Pickaway Co., Ohio. $1\frac{1}{2}$ x $1\frac{1}{4}$.

313 Mammal, polished, of dark purple color, unusually fine and rare; Jersey Co., Ill. $1\frac{1}{2}$ x $1\frac{1}{4}$.

314 Mammal, breast shape, top perforated, extremely fine and of obvious use. Rhea Co., Tenn. $1\frac{1}{2}$ x 1.

315 Mammal, in form a truncated cone, polished, of gray hematite; Polk Co., Tenn. $1\frac{1}{2}$ x $1\frac{1}{2}$.

316 Mammal of slate, nearly the density of hematite, base partly perforated like No. 314; Macon Co., N. C. $1\frac{1}{2}$ x 1.

317 Hematite Ball, unpolished; Mason Co., W. Va. $1\frac{1}{2}$ x $1\frac{1}{2}$.

318 Paint stone of hematite, a fine specimen; Tarentum, Pa. $2\frac{1}{2}$ x 2.

319 Semi-globular object of hematite, unwrought; M. Tenn. $1\frac{1}{2}$ x 1.

320 Another object like the last, partly polished, fine; Middle Tenn. $1\frac{1}{2}$ x 1.

321 Partially grooved Celt of brown hematite, only partly wrought; Missouri. $2\frac{1}{2}$ x 2.

322   Hematite paint stone, partly finished; Lincoln Co., Tenn. 3 x 1½.

323   Paint stone of hematite ; Martin Co., Ky. 2½ x 1.

324   Hematite Marker in unfinished condition ; Western N. C. 2½ x 1.

325   Round hematite Marker, pencil shaped ; Rhea Co., Tenn. 3½ x 1½.

326   Plumb-bob of hematite, one end perforated, surface smooth, partly polished ; Putnam Co., Tenn. 3½ x 1¼.

327   Hematite Plumb-bob, end grooved for suspension, polished, fine and rare ; Missouri. 1½ x 1.

328   Polished Cone or sinker, grooved near the end ; Franklin Co., Ohio. 1½ x 1.

329   Target stone, may be balanced and stood on one end for shooting at with arrows for practice, brown hematite, very fine, and will admit of a fine polish ; Sevier Co., E. Tenn. 2½ x 2.

330   Target stone, one end square at the base ; like the last would admit of a fine polish ; Macon Co., N. C. 2 x 1½.

331   Target stone, a double cone of dark hematite ; W. Va., 1½ x 1.

332   Target stone, one end flattened, hematite, fine ; Rhea Co., N. C. 1¾ x 1½.

333   Target stone of hematite, fine though not nicely wrought; Milton Co., Ga. 1½ x 1½.

334   Target stone, variegated hematite, a most unusual form and material ; N. C. 2 x ½.

335   Target stone of red hematite ; Gwinnett Co., Ga. 2 x 1½.

336   Target stone of red hematite, unpolished ; Middle Tenn. 2 x 1½.

337   Target stone of dark hematite, like the last, unpolished ; N. C. 1½ x 1½.

338   A Ball of unpolished hematite, a target stone ; Middle Tenn. ½ in. dia.

339   Target stone of hematite ; Rhea Co., Tenn. 1½ in. dia.

340   Cone or Mammal of ribbon slate, polished and fine ; Western N. C. 2 x 1.

341   Another Cone of slate, polished, fine ; Mason Co., Va. 2 x 1.

342   Cone of ribbon slate ; Clay Co., N. C. 1½ x 1.

343   Chlorite Cone, fine ; Mason Co., N. C.   1½ x 1.
344   Hemisphere of diorite.   2 x 1.
345   Oval polished stone from an Indian grave ; Clay Co.,
      N. C.   1½ x 1.

AMULETS.

Articles thus designated by Archaeologists, are amongst the most
beautiful of prehistoric relics, being finely wrought and the material
frequently of exquisite beauty. A group of such objects reminds one of
a nest of weasels or little puppies, which they much resemble. The most
striking peculiarity is the transverse perforation at each extremity. They
are sometimes called Saddle stones, or Bird stones, of which forms they
are strikingly suggestive. Nearly all of the finest of these objects are
from Ohio.

346   Amulet of ribbon slate, highly polished, excessively
      rare ; Champaign Co., Ohio.   7 x 2.
347   Amulet of ribbon slate, polished ; Allen Co., Ohio.
      5½ x 2.
348   Amulet of dark brownish slate ; from Greenwich, Huron
      Co., Ohio.   4½ x 2.
349   Amulet of brownish slate, like hematite, very rare form,
      the nose being blunt instead of elongated as generally
      found ; Oneida Co., N. Y.   5½ x 1½.
350   Amulet, long, arching neck ; Wyandotte Co., Ohio.
      4½ x 2.
351   Amulet of ribbon slate, uncommonly fine ; Oneida Co.,
      N. Y.   6 x 1.
352   Amulet, the head resembles a tortoise, the body that
      of a duck ; of ribbon slate, extremely fine ; Allen
      Co., Ohio.   4½ x 1½.
353   Amulet of duck and bird form, of ribbon slate, very
      fine ; Darke Co., Ohio.   4 x 1½.
354   Amulet of dark slate, neck elongated, very graceful ;
      Hamilton Co., Ohio.   4½ x 2.
355   Amulet, much like the last, but head less pointed ;
      Pickaway Co., Ohio.   5 x 2.
356   Amulet of ribbon slate, eyes much enlarged and promi-
      nent. one eye broken ; near Allica, Seneca Co., Ohio.
      5 x 2.

357 Amulet of ribbon slate, polished, fine, head broken off; Jefferson Co., N. Y. 4 x 2.

358 Amulet of brown slate, fine and very rare ; Morrow Co., Ohio. $4\frac{1}{2}$ x $1\frac{1}{2}$.

359 Amulet of light slate, fine ; Hillsdale Co., Mich. 4 x 2.

360 Amulet of ribbon slate ; Richland Co., Ohio. $3\frac{1}{2}$ x 1.

361 Small Amulet of ribbon slate, fine, but broken and repaired ; Wyandotte Co., Ohio. $3\frac{1}{4}$ x 1.

362 Bar Amulet of grey slate, with two pointed ends ; Jefferson Co., N. Y. 4 x 1.

363 Bar Amulet of rare form ; Knox Co., Ohio. $4\frac{1}{2}$ x 1.

364 Bar Amulet, of hematite, a purple colored stone, fine, long and rare ; Allen Co., Ohio. 6 x 1.

365 Bar Amulet of dark slate, the back raised ; E. Ohio. 4 x 1.

366 Small Amulet, or saddle stone, made of hematite ; Chariton Co., Mo.

367 Small bar Amulet, of dark stone, has one perforation ; Macon Co., N. C.

368 Amulet, partly finished but incomplete, has been broken but recently mended ; near Peru, Ind. $6\frac{1}{2}$ x $2\frac{1}{2}$.

CANOE OR BOAT–SHAPED OBJECTS.

These objects following are finely made and very rare.

369 Canoe-shaped object ; bottom has no keel and no perforation ; of dark nearly black slate ; Chala, Yell Co., Ark. 4 x $1\frac{1}{4}$.

370 Boat-shaped object ; double perforation through the body ; of handsome ribbon slate ; Fenton, Wood Co., Ohio. $3\frac{1}{4}$ x $1\frac{1}{2}$.

371 Canoe or boat-shaped object ; of syenite, groove partly imperfect ; Fairfield Co., S. C. $3\frac{1}{2}$ x 2.

372 Canoe-shaped object ; depression semi-globular ; of dark red slate or pottery, no perforations in the bottom ; Cooper Co., Mo. $2\frac{1}{2}$ x $1\frac{1}{2}$.

373 Boat-formed object, with keel and double perforation, polished and very fine ; Morristown, E. Tenn. 3 x 1. (A note sold with the object states that Mr. Hiller, the former owner, had been offered and refused $50 for this article.)

374 Canoe -shaped object, of slate ; resembles No. 372, and like that, has no perforations in the bottom, the depressions being like that, semi-globular ; very fine and handsomely made ; Meade Co., Ky. 2½ x 1¼.

375 Canoe-shaped object, with two perforations, perforations starting from both sides ; Hightower River, Cherokee Co., Ga. 2¾ x 1½.

376 Canoe-shaped object, of brown stone, fine ; Clay Co., N. C. 2 x 1.

377 Canoe-shaped object ; has long keel extending from one end to the other, with transverse perforation ; appears to be of chlorite or green mica slate ; Sharp Mountain Creek, Cherokee Co., Ga. 3 x 1.

378 Canoe-shaped object ; bottom flat, imperforate, tapers endwise from top to bottom ; Dallas Co., Arkansas. 3 x 1¼.

379 Canoe-shaped object ; two large perforations, but has no marked depression ; appears to be of slate ; Huron Co., Ohio. 3 x 1.

380 Canoe-shaped object ; two perforations with one depression ; Swaine Co., N. C. 3 x 1.

381 Canoe-shaped object ; slate or sandstone ; from Upper Island, above Freedom, Beaver Co., Pa. 3½ x 1.

382 Canoe-shaped object, no depression or cavity ; in color and appearance resembles hematite ; Montgomery Co., Miss. 3 x 1.

383 Canoe-shaped object of hematite ; Montgomery Co., Miss.

384 Canoe-shaped object ; resembles hematite ; no depression or perforation ; Montgomery Co., Miss. 3 x 1.

385 Object of slate, canoe-shaped, but without keel or depression ; Meade Co., Ky. 3½ x 1.

386 Long elliptical object, approaching canoe-shape, but without depression ; Breckenridge Co., Ky. 4¾ x 1.

387 Canoe-shaped object, in form like a double pointed cigar, two perforations ; North Carolina. 4 x 1.

388 Canoe-shaped object, of nearly black diorite ; ends blunt, no perforations ; Meade Co., Ky. 4¼ x 1.

389 Canoe-shaped object, sides notched, no depression ; No. Carolina. 3½ x ¾.

390 Canoe-shaped object, with depression or perforations ; of quartzite, fine ; Tenn. 2¾ x ¾.

391 Canoe-shaped object, longitudinal depression extending from end to end, one partly finished perforation ; sand stone ; Mercer Co., Ohio. 2¼ x 1¼.

392 Elliptical canoe-shaped stone, of slate ; Lincoln Co., Tenn. 4½ x 1.

393 Prehistoric relics found at Mound City, consisting of pottery and a number of human bones ; amongst them is easily recognized the humerus, or large bone of the arm, also portions of the skull and jaw, and several objects of stone, probably agricultural implements.

394 Prehistoric Stone, probably attached to a handle by raw hide, and used as a hammer, partly polished by use.

CELTS, AXES, BEADS, ETC.

The following Objects including numbers from 395 to 410 are from a Mound in Jefferson Co., East Tennessee.

395 Ungrooved Axe of ribbon slate ; without exception the finest polished ungrooved axe I have ever seen. 9x3.

396 Ungrooved Axe of dark, nearly black slate, polished nearly all over ; almost equal to the last. 8 x 3.

397 Celt, of dark slate, nearly all polished. 4½ x 2½.

398 Agricultural implement, oval, polished, of dark gray slate ; has cutting edge nearly all round ; very fine and rare. 8 x 4.

399 Spear head, in shape nearly dagger form, fine and rare. 7½ x 2.

400 Discoidal stone of quartzite, double convex, very fine. 2 in. dia.

401 Another double convex Discoidal, of polished, dark stone. 1¾ in. dia.

402 Two small discoidal stones ; equally fine, but smaller than the preceding. 2 pcs.

403 Thin Breast plates of native copper, from the mound mentioned ; a rare lot. 7 pcs., from 1 to 5 in. square.

404 Wooden Buttons, supposed to have been used with the preceding plates, preserved with the salts of copper in the mound from the plates of which they formed a part. 2 pcs.

405 Fragment of a Mound builder's Pipe. 2 x 1¾.

406 Beads made from the columella of the conch shell. 8 pieces.

407 Beads, similar to last, average smaller, all fine. 12 pcs.
408 Shell Beads, smaller than the last, but still of large size.
32 pcs.
409 Shell Beads, in various forms, flattened, elongated, etc.
92 pcs.
410 Shell Beads, form similar to last. 100 pcs.

The following objects to No. 420 are all from a mound in Montgomery Co., Arkansas, and all were found together.

410a Fine Celt, edge partly polished. 6½ x 3.
411 Another of the same form, long, ovate. 5 x 2.
412 Polished implement, nearly hemispherical, of dark color. 2½ in. dia.
413 Flat, polished, and nearly hemispherical stone. 2 x 1½.
414 Mound builder's Pipe, of pottery, odd in form, bowl discolored by smoking. 2 x 2.
415 Mound builder's Pipe of pottery, covered with lozenge-shaped ornaments; broken. 3 x 2.
416 Another pottery Pipe without the ornamentation; broken. 3 x 1½.
417 Another mound Pipe bearing marks of ancient burning in a kiln. 2 x 1.
418 Round Ball or hammer stone, plainly marked or clipped; a good specimen. 2¼ in. dia.
419 Beads made from the columella of the conch shell; these beads are of various lengths, from ¾ to 1½ in.; all are perforated. 8 pcs.
420 Fragments of bones showing part of the jaw containing a number of double teeth. 6 pcs.

DISCOIDALS.

The following lots to No. 519, comprise Mr. Spang's immense collection of Discoidal Stones, which with his former lot purchased by me several years ago made the finest collection extant. They may now be found entire in the collection of Mr. A. E. Douglas, of New York City.

421 Bi-concave Discoidal, as fine as though turned in a lathe; the bi-concave saucer-like depressions are supplemented by the addition of a pair of smaller depressions fairly in the centre of the same; these last are half-bullet shaped; the material is of stone resembling cheese or rather butter. 5½ in. dia., cavities ⅝ in. deep; E. Tennessee.

422 Double concave Discoidal ; the interior depressions in this object are larger than the last described and equally fine. 6 in. dia.

423 Bi-concave Discoidal, of veined and colored stone ; a fine and beautiful object. 5 in. dia.

424 Bi-concave Discoidal, the concavities in this stone are like No. 421. The material is similar to last, and though much worn is unblemished ; Alabama. 5 in. diameter.

425 Bi-concave Discoidal, of dark colored granite, marked by Mr. Spang "pudding stone ; " Sevier Co., E. Tenn. 4½ in. dia.

426 Bi-concave Discoidal, of dark colored stone, resembling quartzite ; Sevier Co., Tenn. 5½ in. dia.

427 Bi-concave Discoidal, of dark, nearly black stone ; Rhea Co., Tenn. 5 in. Dia.

428 Bi-concave Discoidal, of nearly white stone, perforated, finely made, of extreme hardness ; E. Tenn. 5 in. dia.

429 Bi-concave Discoidal ; has supplementary depressions in the bottom of the saucer-shaped ones. Material similar to No. 422 ; N. C. 4½ in. dia.

430 Variegated bi-concave Discoidal ; Chattahoochee River, Milton Co., Ga. 4½ in. dia.

431 Double concaved Discoidal ; discolored from much use ; Rhea Co., Tenn. 4 in. dia.

432 Bi-concave Discoidal ; nearly black, polished ; Macon Co., N. C. 3½ in. dia.

433 Bi-concave Discoidal, of very hard reddish granite ; this stone is finely made and with great labor ; Jersey Co., Ill. 4 in. dia., 2¼ in. thick.

434 Bi-concave Discoidal, of white quartz or chalcedony, a rare material, very large ; Cumberland Co., Ky. 6 in. dia.

435 Double concaved Discoidal, of the form known as cheese shaped. The fine series of stones of this form in Mr. Spang's former collection is unmatched. The largest in the catalogue. Burkville, Cumberland Co., Ky. 6 in. dia., 4 in. thick.

436 Double concave Discoidal ; material like annato-colored cheese, depressions of medium depth ; Chattanooga, Tenn. 3½ in. dia.

437 Double concave Discoidal, dark color, nearly black, large depressions extending through the centre ; Pepin Co., Wisconsin. 2½ in. dia.

438 Triangular double concaved Discoidal, two small depressions ; Macon Co., N. C. Sides 3 in. long.

439 Bi-concave Discoidal, edges equidistant and parallel, a finely polished and handsome stone ; Lincoln Co., 2 in. dia.

440 Bi-concave Discoidal, of light granite, well formed and an unusual shape ; Western N. C. 4 x 3.

441 Bi-concave Discoidal, of dark granite ; Beaver Valley, Pa. 4 in. dia.

442 Bi-concave Discoidal, cheese shape, fine and a very rare form, much less common than the thin ones ; Lincoln Co., Middle Tenn. 3 in. dia., 2 in. thick.

443 Bi-concave Discoidal, depressions less marked than usual, but a fine stone ; Allegheny Co., Pa. 3½ in. dia.

444 Bi-concave Discoidal, of reddish granite, concavities less pronounced than usual ; Sevier Co., Tenn. 3½ in. dia.

445 Bi-concave Discoidal, of unusual variegated granite of black and light material ; Beaver Co., Pa. 2½ in. dia.

446 Bi-concave Discoidal, material like the last ; from Franklin Co., Mo. 2½ in. dia.

447 Bi-concave Discoidal, slight depressions ; N. Georgia.

448 Bi-concave Discoidal, may be of mound pottery ; Massac Co., Ill. 2 in. dia.

449 Bi-concave Discoidal, of dark granite, from Beaver Co., Pa. 2½ in. dia.

450 Bi-concave Discoidal ; Tischomingo Co., Miss. 2½ in. dia.

451 Bi-concave Discoidal, rude ; Lincoln Co., Tenn. 2¼ in. dia.

452 Bi-concave Discoidal, slight depressions, of sandstone ; Meigs Co., Tenn. 2 in. dia.

453 Bi-concave Discoidal, perforated through the centre; appears to be of slate , Douglas Co., Oregon. 3 x 2½ inches.

454 Bi-concave Discoidal, with large circular perforation ; James Co., Tenn. 1¾ in. dia.

455 Bi-concave Discoidal, large perforation through the centre ; Knox Co., Tenn. 1¾ in. dia.

456 Bi-concave Discoidal, with large central perforation; Rhea Co., Tenn. 1½ in. dia.

457 Bi-concave Discoidal, small, but of fine workmanship; Tower River, N. C.

458 Bi-concave Discoidals of small size, fine, from 1 in. to 1½ in. dia.; various localities.

459 Perforated bi-concave Discoidal; Massac Co., Ill. 1½ in. dia.

460 Double concave Discoidal. The perforation through this stone appears to be natural; Newago Co., Mich. 3½ in. dia.

461 Bi-concave Discoidal; like the last the perforation through this stone appears to be a natural formation, but it is nevertheless a very fine one; Breckenridge Co., Ky. 3 in. dia.

462 Bi-concave Discoidal; Middle Tenn. 2½ in. dia.

463 Bi-concave Discoidal, rudely made; Pulaski Co., Ill. 3 in. dia.

464 Bi-concave Discoidal, of black diorite. 2½ in. dia.

465 Bi-concave Discoidal, of reddish stone; Lincoln Co., Tenn. 2 in. dia.

466 Double convex Discoidal, of chalcedony, a rare material for so large a stone: Lincoln Co., Tenn. 5 in. dia.

467 Double convex Discoidal, of quartzite; Western N. C. 4½ in. dia.

468 Another fine bi-convex Discoidal of quartzite; Macon Co., N. C. 4 in. dia.

469 Discoidal stone, surface plano-convex; Macon Co., S. West N. C. 4½ in. dia.

470 Plano-convex Discoidal; Montgomery Co., Miss. 4 in. diameter.

471 Bi-convex Discoidal, of white quartzite; Macon Co., N. C. 3½ in. dia.

472 Plano-convex Discoidal, of dark colored ingrained stone; Massac Co., Ill. 4 in. dia.

473 Bi-convex Discoidal, of fine ornamental stone resembling quartzite; N. C. 3½ in.

474 Bi-convex Discoidal; Macon Co., N. C. 3½ in. dia.

475 Bi-convex Discoidal, of black stone like diorite; No. Carolina. 3 in. dia.

476 Plano-convex Discoidal, of granite; No. Carolina. 3 in. dia.

477 Bi-convex Discoidal, nicely polished ; Caledonia, Pulaski Co., So. Ill. 2½ in. dia.

478 Bi-convex Discoidal, of chalcedony, polished and fine ; Sevier Co., Tenn. 2½ in. dia.

479 Bi-convex Discoidal, of chalcedony, veined and polished, fine and rare ; E. Tenn. 2 in. dia.

480 Bi-convex Discoidal, of quartz or quartzite ; has a small piece shattered from one side, but very fine ; Macon Co., N. C. 2¼ in. dia.

481 Bi-convex Discoidal, fine ; from an island in the Tennessee River, Meigs Co., Tenn. 2¼ in. dia.

482 Bi-convex Discoidal, nearly black ; Rhea Co., Tenn. 2 in. dia.

483 Discoidal, like the last in form and color, Chattooga River, Rabun Co., Ga. 1¾ in. dia.

484 Bi-concave Discoidal, of quartzite ; Rhea Co., Tenn. 1½ in. dia.

485 Bi-convex Discoidal, of quartzite ; Polk Co., Tenn. 1½ in. dia.

486 Bi-convex Discoidal, of quartzite ; has been used on one side as a mortar ; Rhea Co., Tenn. 2 in. dia.

487 Bi-convex Discoidal of quartzite ; Gwinnett Co., Ga. 1½ in. dia.

488 Bi-convex Discoidal of quartzite, fine ; Rhea Co., Tenn. 1½ in. dia.

489 Bi-convex Discoidal of quartzite ; Sevier Co., Tenn. 1½ in. dia.

490 Bi-convex Discoidal ; from near Sharpsburg, Allegheny Co., Pa. 3 in. dia.

491 Bi-concave Discoidal, of limestone, rude ; Lodi, Miss. 2¼ in. dia.

492 Bung-shaped Discoidal, veined or clouded quartzite ; near Tenn. line, N. Ga. 3½ in. dia.

493 Discoidal, bung-shaped, of quartzite ; Clay Co., N. C. 2½ in. dia.

494 Discoidal, bung-shaped, of quartzite ; Western N. C. 3½ in. dia.

495 Discoidal, bung-shaped, of dark stone, veined ; Meigs Co., Tenn. 3 in. dia.

496 Discoidal, bung-shaped, of quartzite, very handsome and finely wrought ; Swaine Co., N. C. 2½ in. dia.

497 Discoidal, bung-shaped, of variegated quartzite, fine; Clay Co., N. C. 2¼ in. dia.

498 Discoidal, bung-shaped, of dark stone, fine; South Western North Carolina. 2½ in.

499 Discoidal, bung-shaped, of quartzite; Swaine Co. N. C. 3 in. dia.

500 Discoidal, bung-shaped, of veined quartzite; Macon Co., N. C. 2½ in. dia.

501 Bung-shaped Discoidal of quartzite, and nicely wrought; Macon Co., N. C. 2½ in. dia.

502 Bung-shaped Discoidal, of dark, handsome stone; from Northern Ga. 3 in. dia.

503 Black Discoidal, bung-shaped; Macon Co., N. C. 3 in. diameter.

504 Black Discoidal, bung-shaped; Macon Co., N. C. 2¾ in. dia.

505 Discoidal, bung-shaped, of light greyish slate; Rabun Co., N. Ga. 3 in. dia.

506 Bung-shaped Discoidal, nearly black; from S. West No. Carolina. 2¾ in. dia.

507 Bung-shaped Discoidal; Swaine Co., N. C. 2½ in. dia.

508 Bung-shaped Discoidal, nearly black; Macon Co., N. C. 2½ in. dia.

510 Bung-shaped Discoidal, dark, nearly black; Rabun Co., N. Ga. 2¼ in. dia.

511 Bung-shaped Discoidal, smooth and of dark color; S. W. No. Carolina. 2 in. dia.

512 Bung-shaped Discoidal, like coarse sandstone; Rabun Co., Ga. 2¼ in. dia.

513 Bung-shaped bi-convex Discoidal; Macon Co., N. C. 2½ in. dia.

514 Cheese-shaped bi-concave Discoidal, in depth equal to its width, very fine and rare; Lincoln Co., M. Tenn. 3½ in. dia.

515 Discoidal of plano-convex form, precisely resembles a mass of maple sugar just taken from the boiling pot, and presents a most appetizing appearance; Pulaski Co., Ill. 3 in, dia.

516 Concavo-convex Discoidal, resembles a natural formation; Lincoln Co., M. Tenn. 3¾ in. dia.

517 Discs, various forms, bi-convex and bi-concave; different localities in Tenn., and various sizes. 6 pcs.

518 A similar lot from various localities ; a pretty selection·
18 pcs.

519 A wrought object of quartzite, in shape resembling the
hoof of a young colt ; shows the frog very plainly.

520 Object of shell, made from univalve shell from the Atlantic coast, a skimmer or ladle, polished, with two
small perforations ; Solomon Islands. 6 x 7.

521 A similar object, polished on both sides, one large and
two smaller perforations ; Rhea Co., Tenn. 3½ in. dia.

522 A similar object, formed from an oyster shell ; outside
shows the outer coating of the shell, two perforations ;
from a mound 18 miles above Knoxville, E. Tenn.
5 x 4.

523 Large skimmer-shaped object, both interior and exterior
show original coating. A carved figure, represented
by eyes, nose and mouth, is evidently meant for an
Indian ; 3 perforations ; from same mound as No. 522.
7½ x 5½.

524 Hair Pins or ornaments, carved from oyster shells, each
with a small perforation through the pointed end ;
from the Atlantic Coast.

525 Perforated ornament from an oyster ; Lincoln Co.,
Tenn. 2 in. dia.

526 Small skimmer-shaped shell ; Knox Co., Tenn. 2½ x 1½.

527 Univalve shells; from various localities on the Atlantic
coast. 10 pcs.

528 Fragments of Mound pottery, one a portion of a large
vessel used in salt boiling; Beaver Valley, Beaver
Co., Pa. 4 pcs.

529 Perforated Boss or disc ; found on the site of the old
fort in Pulaski Co., Ill. 4½ in. dia.

530 Fragments of Mound pottery from Florida, two marked
with deeply incised lines. 3 large pcs.

531 Fragments of Mound pottery from Tenn.; all marked
with incised lines. 5 pcs.

532 Fragments of Mound pottery ; from Florida. 40 pcs.

533 Portion of a Mound pottery tray ; from Oneida Co., N.
Y.; two smaller pieces from N. C. 3 pcs.

534 Pieces of cement or clay pavement, a part of a mound
near Decatur, Ala. 3 pcs.

535 Pottery Discs, perforated ; from Montgomery Co., Ala.
4 pcs.

536 Fragments of pottery with incised ornamentation ; from Westport, Ontario, Can. 7 pcs.

537 Discoidal stones, etc., of small size ; mostly from Rhea Co., Tenn. 8 pcs.

538 Small perforated Discoidals; from N. Carolina and Tenn. 4 pcs.

539 Perforated Discs of pottery; from Ohio and Tenn. 4 pcs.

540 Shuttle-shaped Pendant, two rather large-sized perforations ; Beaver Valley, Pa. 6 x 2.

541 Boat-shaped object; has been broken at perforations near both ends, polished, fine ; Huron Co., Ohio. 6 x 1.

542 Banner-stone, shaped like a pair of horns; appears to be of slate; Clay Co., N. C. 2½ x 1.

543 Boat-shaped object; Yadkin River, Montgomery Co., N. C. 2½ x 1¼.

544 A small but handsome Celt, slate, resembles chlorite ; Beaver Co., Pa. 3½ x 1.

545 Object of steatite, appears to be the cover of a dish ; Thom Grove, Tenn. 2½ x 2.

546 Half of a butterfly-shaped Banner stone ; Yadkin River, N. C. 3½ x 2.

547 Prehistoric perforated stone, marked with an ancient carving resembling a bird ; Cumberland Co., Ky. 2 x 1½.

548 Pot Smoother ; an implement believed to have been used in the fabrication of mound pottery ; would serve equally well as a stopper; Danville, Tenn. 2 x 1.

549 An implement, apparently for the same use as No. 548, perforated near the end ; Rhea Co., Tenn. 2 x 1.

550 Two other objects for apparently the same purpose ; from Beaufort, S. C.

551 Paint pot, supposed to be used for the grinding of pigments. 1½ x 1.

552 A Mound pottery object, marked with incised lines ; Florida. 2½ x 1½.

553 Small neatly formed Celt or pendant; Macon Co., N. C. 1½ x 1.

554 Stone Bead or nut, of slate, very large perforation ; N. Carolina. ¾ x ½.

GROOVED AXES.

The following collection of Grooved Axes, Numbers 555 to 769, constitute the finest collection I have ever possessed, or have had the opportunity of examining. They are diverse in form and material, and obtained from all localities where these implements are found in the U. S. and North America. The extreme size is given in inches only.

555 Grooved Axe of light granite, large and handsome; Hancock Co., Ky. 7 x 5½.

556 Grooved Axe, groove broad and deep, point narrow; Ky. 9 x 5.

557 Grooved Axe, with one edge longitudinally grooved, fine; from a mound, La Porte Co., Ind. 7 x 4.

558 Grooved Axe, both edges grooved lengthwise, somewhat imperfect; Cooper Co., Mo. 5 x 3.

559 Grooved Axe, of light-colored coarse granite; North Carolina. 4 x 3.

560 Grooved Axe, head rounded, groove deep; Breckenridge Co., Ky. 7 x 4.

561 Small grooved Axe, of gray, light-colored stone; Rochester, Beaver Co., Pa. 4½ x 3.

562 Grooved Axe of sandstone; N. Carolina. 4 x 2½.

563 Grooved Axe of sandstone; banks of the Ohio River. 3 x 2.

564 Grooved Axe, of dark granite; Massac Co., Ill. 3½ x 3.

565 Grooved Axe of dark granite, polished all over except the edge which has been broken; Cooper Co., Mo. 5½ x 3.

566 Grooved Axe of light diorite, edge narrow and elongated; Clinton Co., Ill. 6 x 5½.

567 Grooved Axe of reddish colored stone, nicely finished, the groove extends lengthwise up one edge; Cooper Co., Mo. 4½ x 2½.

568 Grooved Axe of bluish trap rock; Missouri. 4½ x 3¾.

569 Grooved Axe of light granite; a curious seam appears in its surface; Washington, Ill. 5½ x 4.

570 Grooved Axe of slate; Ky. 4 x 2⅓.

571 Grooved Axe, of small size; Cloverport, Ky. 3 x 2.

572 Grooved Axe of gray stone, polished nearly all over; Ohio Valley, Beaver Co., Pa. 7 x 4.

C 1.10 573 Grooved Axe, large and fine; Franklin Co., Mo.   7½ x 4½.

574 Grooved Axe of small size, but fine ; Ill.   3½ x 2½.

C .37 575 Grooved Axe of coarse mica slate ; Ky.   8 x 4.

576 Grooved Axe, deep, broad groove, head somewhat imperfect ; S. Carolina.   6 x 4.

577 Grooved Axe of sandstone ; Kaskaskia River.   7½ x 4½.

578 Grooved Axe of sandstone ; Kentucky.   3 x 2½.

579 Grooved Axe, groove shallow ; Cooper Co., Mo.   3 x 2.

580 Grooved Axe, ordinary ; Hot Springs, Ark.   4½ x 3½.

581 Grooved Axe of dark granite, bit broken ; Cooper Co., Mo.   6 x 4.

582 Grooved Axe, nearly circular, end broken ; Cooper Co., Mo.   5 x 3½.

583 Grooved Axe of polished diorite ; Ocanio, Ill.   4 x 3.

584 Grooved Axe of light reddish stone ; Macon Co., N. C.   4 x 3.

585 Extra grooved Axe, of dark, nearly black granite ; Cooper Co., Mo.   6½ x 4.

586 Grooved Axe of reddish stone, partly polished ; Breckenridge Co., Ky.   7 x 5.

587 Grooved Axe, with broad, deep groove ; has probably been used as a hoe ; James Co., E. Tenn.   8 x 4.

588 Grooved Axe, grooving broad and deep : of uncommon form ; Union Co., Tenn.   7½ x 4½.

589 Large grooved Axe, partly polished; Missouri. 7½ x 3½.

590 Grooved Axe, with broad shallow groove ; mica slate ; Mercer Co., N. C.   8 x 4.

591 Beautifully polished grooved Axe, of black diorite, groove extends all around and on one side ; extremely fine and rare, I think the finest axe in the Sale ; Cooper Co., Mo.   4 x 2½.

592 Grooved Axe, polished all over, and of stone almost as beautiful as No. 591 ; Huron Co., Ohio.   4½ x 3.

593 Grooved Axe, polished, and nearly equal in beauty to the two last ; material of gray diorite ; Cooper Co., Missouri.   5 x 4.

594 Grooved Axe of fine stone, edge pointed or narrowed; So. Yadkin River, N. C.   5 x 3.

595 Grooved Axe, small but fine ; Breckenridge Co., Ky.   3 x 2.

596 Grooved Axe; Clay Co., S. West No. Carolina. $5\frac{1}{2}$ x $3\frac{1}{2}$.

597 Grooved Axe, with deep, broad groove, of light colored slate; E. Tenn. $4\frac{1}{2}$ x $2\frac{1}{2}$.

598 Grooved Axe of clouded, light and dark stone; Cooper Co., Mo. $3\frac{1}{2}$ x $2\frac{1}{2}$.

599 Large grooved Axe, blade a little damaged, but of fine form; Clay Co., N. C. $6\frac{1}{2}$ x $4\frac{1}{2}$.

600 Grooved Axe, polished nearly all over, fine; Cooper Co., Mo. $3\frac{1}{2}$ x $2\frac{1}{2}$.

601 Grooved Axe, small, narrow groove; Macon Co., N. C. $3\frac{1}{2}$ x $2\frac{1}{2}$.

602 Grooved Axe, edges perpendicular to the flats; of diorite; Cooper Co., Missouri. $5\frac{1}{2}$ x 3.

603 Grooved Axe, one side flattened; Cooper Co., Missouri. $4\frac{1}{2}$ x 3.

604 Grooved Axe of rough stone, well made; Rabun Co., Ga. 4 x $2\frac{1}{2}$.

605 Grooved Axe, shaped like a canoe; Breckenridge Co., Ky. $5\frac{1}{2}$ x 3.

606 Grooved Axe, partly polished; Breckenridge Co., Ky. $4\frac{1}{2}$ x $2\frac{1}{2}$.

607 Grooved Axe, partly polished; Cooper Co., Missouri. $4\frac{1}{2}$ x $2\frac{1}{2}$.

608 Grooved Axe of light granite, broad deep groove, partly polished; Mason Co., Va. $5\frac{1}{2}$ x $2\frac{1}{2}$.

609 Grooved Axe, broad and deep groove; resembles the common axe of Arizona; blade broken short off near the groove; Cooper Co., Missouri. 4 x $3\frac{1}{2}$.

610 Short grooved Axe, irregular in form; Licking Co., Va. 4 x 3.

611 Grooved Axe, groove broad and deep; Cooper Co., Mo. $4\frac{1}{2}$ x $2\frac{1}{2}$.

612 Grooved Axe, groove broad; another groove extends along one edge; Ralls Co., Mo. $3\frac{1}{2}$ x 2.

613 Grooved Axe, nicely finished and partly polished; Cooper Co., Mo. $4\frac{1}{2}$ x $2\frac{1}{2}$.

614 Grooved Axe, edge also grooved, polished, of grey stone; M. B., Ky. 5 x $3\frac{1}{2}$.

615 Grooved Axe of dark coarse granite, a portion of the material seems to be black schorl. $4\frac{1}{2}$ x 3.

616 Grooved Axe of dark stone ; Hawkins Co., Tenn. 5 x 2½.

617 Grooved Axe, nicely finished ; Rabun Co., Ga. 5½ x 3½.

618 Grooved Axe of granite, head rounded ; Franklin Co., Missouri. 6 x 3.

619 Grooved Axe, partly polished ; Hancock Co., Ky. 4½ x 2.

620 Grooved Axe, polished ; Breckenridge Co., Ky. 3½ x 2.

621 Grooved Axe, partly polished ; Montgomery Co., Ark. 5 x 2½.

622 Grooved Axe, head elongated ; West Liberty, Jasper Co., Ill. 4½ x 2.

623 Grooved Axe, resembles hematite which it is not ; the head shows a new fracture. 4½ x 2½.

624 Grooved Axe, with elongated point ; rude ; Montgomery Co., Ark. 4 x 3.

625 Grooved Axe, of light stone or quartzite, groove shallow ; Breckenridge Co., Ky. 4 x 3.

626 Grooved Axe, of black and white diorite intermingled ; Michigan. 4 x 2½.

627 Grooved Axe, partly polished ; Cooper Co. Mo. 5½ x 3.

628 Grooved Axe, head diagonally grooved, of dark granite, bitt much elongated ; a finely made axe ; E. Tenn. 6 x 3.

629 Grooved Axe, approaches circular, an unusual form ; Hawkins Co., Tenn. 3½ x 3½.

630 Grooved Axe, of sandstone ; Hancock Co., Ky. 4½ x 2½.

631 Grooved Axe ; Clay Co., N. C. 3½ x 3.

632 Grooved Axe, of granite, head shortened ; Turnbull Co., Ohio. 5 x 3½.

633 Grooved Axe, a common form, fine ; from Cooper Co., Mo. 5 x 3.

634 Grooved Axe of black diorite : Beaver Co., Pa. 3½ x 2½.

635 Grooved Axe, resembles the grooved axe of Arizona, very fine ; Cooper Co., Mo. 5½ x 4.

636 Grooved Axe, edge grooved, a fine axe ; Franklin Co., Mo. 5½ x 4.

637 Grooved Axe, shows signs of disintegration ; Macon Co., N. C. 6 x 4.

638 Small grooved Axe, partly polished ; Ky. 3 x 2.

639 Another small grooved Axe ; Vigo Co., Ind. 3½ x 2.

640 Grooved Axe, of light granite ; Clement, Ill. 5 x 3½.

641 Grooved Axe, has an uncommonly broad groove ;
Cooper Co., Mo. 4½ x 2½.

642 Grooved Axe, of gouge form, polished, fine and rare ;
James Co., E. Tenn. 5 x 2.

643 Grooved Axe of characteristic Missouri form ; the groove
extends round the head and on both edges ; polished,
a very fine object ; McLean Co., Ill. 6½ x 4½.

644 Large grooved Axe, nearly circular, of light granite ;
Pulaski Co., Ill. 6 x 4½.

645 Grooved Axe, similar to No. 643, a fine form : Jackson
Co., Mo. 5½ x 3.

646 Grooved Axe. This implement resembles a digging
tool, and was doubtless used in agriculture. A finely
formed implement; Rhea Co., Tenn. 10½ x 4½.

647 Large grooved Axe. The groove has a ridge on both
sides; Morristown, Tenn. 8 x 5.

648 Grooved Axe, in form resembles No. 647 ; Union Co.,
Tenn. 5 x 3.

649 Grooved Axe of coarse granite; large but rude ; S. W.
N. Carolina. 8½ x 5.

650 Grooved Axe of sandstone, groove surrounding the
head : Macon Co., N. C. 5 x 3.

651 Grooved Axe, partly polished ; Huron Co., Ohio. 5
x 3.

652 Grooved Axe, large and finely made, has been polished ;
bitt broken ; Hawkins Co., Tenn. 9 x 6.

653 Deeply grooved Axe of the Missouri pattern ; Fond du
Lac, Wis. 5 x 3.

654 Grooved Axe, the rock plentifully supplied with small
garnets : N. C. 4½ x 3½.

655 Grooved Axe, one face polished ; Mo. 6 x 3.

656 Grooved Axe of the Missouri pattern, bitt broken ; Mo.
4½ x 3.

657 Grooved Axe, deeply grooved and notched on one edge ;
Fond du Lac, Wis. 6 x 3½.

658 Thick, short, grooved Axe, marked with white veins;
Mo. 4 x 4.

659 Grooved Axe of dark reddish stone, declared by the
finder to be different from any he has ever seen,
though the location was one abounding in stone axes ;
Cooper Co., Mo. 3½ x 2½.

660   Small, fine grooved Axe of sandstone; Rabun Co., Ga.
  5 x 3.

661   Small, handsomely polished grooved Axe of granite;
  Cooper Co., Mo.   3½ x 2.

662   Very small grooved Axe, of diorite; E. Tenn.   2¼ x 2.

663   Thin, long, grooved Axe, probably used in mound
  building: Chattooga River, Ga. One side polished, a
  very fine and rare implement.   9 x 3½.

664   Grooved Axe of reddish stone, surface disintegrated;
  partly polished; Breckinridge Co., Ky.   6 x 3¼.

665   Grooved Axe, the surface covered with dark crystal, and
  several veins running through the substance of the
  stone.   6 x 3¼.

_C_ — 50666   Grooved Axe of light colored granite; Hawkins Co.,
  Tenn.   6 x 3¼.

667   Grooved Axe of sharp grained light sandstone, head
  square: Franklin Co., Mo.   5¼ x 3.

668   Grooved Axe of diorite, one side polished the other
  somewhat chipped; Cooper Co., Mo.   4¼ x 3.

669   Grooved Axe of light sandstone : S. Carolina.   5 x 3.

670   Grooved Axe of variegated stone, varying from light to
  dark, partly polished; Franklin Co., Mo.   6 x 3.

671   Grooved Axe, same variety of stone as No. 670; Chariton Co., Mo.   4 x 2½.

672   Grooved Axe of light colored sandstone; N. Carolina.
  5 x 3.

673   Grooved Axe, groove polished, short and wide, a rare
  form; Hawkins Co., Tenn.   5 x 5.

674   Grooved Axe, similar to No. 673; Mo.   5½ x 4½.

675   Grooved Axe of chert, shows much of the natural wear
  of the stone; Middle Ky.   5 x 3½.

676   Small grooved Axe; Hancock Co., Ky.   3 x 2½.

677   Grooved Axe of short grained sandstone; Hancock Co.,
  Ky.   4½ x 3.

678   Small grooved Axe of granite; Cumberland Co., Ky.
  4 x 2½.

679   Small grooved Axe of chert ; Louisa Co., Va.   3½ x 2.

680   Small grooved Axe of dark slate ; Breckenridge Co.,
  Ky.   3 x 2.

681   Grooved Axe of green slate ; Dorchester Co., Md.   5½
  x 3½.

682   Grooved Axe of dark granite ; Clay Co., N. C.   5½ x 4.

683   Grooved Axe of dark slate ; Potosi, Mo.   5 x 3.

684   Polished grooved Axe of the Missouri form ; Cooper Co., Mo.   5½ x 3½.

685   Grooved Axe of dark sandstone ; Calhoun Co., Ill.   3½ x 3.

686   Grooved Axe of sandstone ; Hot Springs Co., Ark.   4½ x 2½.

687   Grooved Axe of coarse grained granite ; Randolph Co., Ill.   7 x 1.

688   Grooved Axe of dark, nearly black granite ; Franklin Co., Mo.   6 x 4.

689   Grooved Axe, end nearly pointed ; Breckenridge Co., Ky.   6 x 4.

690   Grooved Axe, partly polished ; Breckenridge Co., Ky.   7 x 3.

691   Grooved Axe ; Cooper Co., Mo.   5 x 4.

692   Small coarse grained grooved Axe ; N. C.   3 x 3.

693   Grooved Axe of coarse stone, oval ; Chariton, Co., Mo.   5 x 3½.

694   Grooved Axe of slate ; Breckenridge Co., Ky.   6 x 4.

695   Grooved Axe, rude ; Breckenridge Co., Ky.   5 x 3½.

696   Grooved Axe, head pointed ; James Co., E. Tenn.   4½ x 2½.

697   Grooved Axe, hammer-shaped ; Breckenridge Co., Ky.   5 x 3.

698   Grooved Axe, edge fractured ; Breckenridge Co., Ky.   5½ x 3½.

699   Small grooved Axe ; Rabun Co., Ga.   4 x 3.

700   Grooved Axe of slate, has been used as a whetstone ; form elongated ; Rhea Co., Tenn.   7½ x 2½.

701   Grooved Axe, flat and thin ; Breckenridge Co., Ky.   4½ x 4.

702   Grooved Axe of diorite, grooved also on one edge ; Finney Co., Kan.   4 x 3.

703   Grooved Axe, broad deep groove and partly polished ; Huron Co., Ohio.   5 x 3.

704   Grooved Axe of light-colored sandstone, end pointed or narrowed ; Breckenridge Co., Ky.   8 x 5.

705   Grooved Axe, head unusually broad, point narrow ; Lancaster, Pa.   6½ x 4.

706   Grooved Axe, broad, deep groove; Clay Co., Ky. $4\frac{1}{2}$ x 4.

707   Grooved Axe of sandstone; Breckenridge Co., Ky. $4\frac{1}{2}$ x 3.

708   Grooved Axe of sharp grained, dark-colored stone; Beaver Co., Pa. 6 x $3\frac{1}{2}$.

709   Grooved Axe, rude, of slate; Breckenridge Co., Ky. 4 x $2\frac{1}{2}$.

710   Grooved Axe of light-colored, nearly white stone; Bendton, Ark. 5 x 2.

711   Grooved Axe, sides perpendicular to its flats; Calhoun Co., Ill. $5\frac{1}{2}$ x $2\frac{1}{2}$.

712   Grooved Axe, reddish stone, in part polished; Breckenridge Co., Ky. 4 x $2\frac{1}{2}$.

713   Grooved Axe, edges partly polished; Illinois. 5 x 3.

714   Grooved Axe, surface partly polished; Breckenridge Co., Ky. 5 x $2\frac{1}{2}$.

715   Grooved Axe, nearly square, of sandstone; Lancaster Co., Pa. $6\frac{1}{2}$ x $3\frac{1}{2}$.

716   Small grooved Axe, edges also grooved, partly polished; a handsome material; Muscatine Co., Ia., 3 x 2.

717   Grooved Axe of black diorite or granite; Middle Mo. 5 x 3.

718   Grooved Axe of coarse red stone; E. Tenn. 4 x $3\frac{1}{2}$.

719   Grooved Axe, roughly made; Breckenridge Co., Ky. 4 x 3.

720   Grooved Axe, rectangular, partly polished; Cooper Co., Mo. 4 x $2\frac{1}{2}$.

721   Grooved Axe or hammer, resembles hematite which it is not; Carter Co., Tenn. 4 x 2.

722   Grooved Axe of the usual Missouri form, edges flat, polished; a fine axe. Cooper Co., Mo. 4 x 3.

723   Grooved Axe of dark reddish granite; Cooper Co., Mo. 4 x 3.

724   Grooved Axe, called by the finder "a hoe"; polished nearly all over; Missouri River, Cooper Co., Mo. $4\frac{1}{2}$ x 3.

725   Grooved Axe, of reddish stone, weathered and worn; Lawrence Co., Ind. 5 x 3.

726   Small grooved Axe, partly polished; Breckenridge Co., Ky. 3 x 2.

727 Grooved Axe, more nearly polished than the last; Ky. 3 x 2.

728 Grooved Axe of light granite ; Breckenridge Co., Ky. 3½ x 3.

729 Grooved Axe, edges flat, polished all over, a fine implement ; Breckenridge Co., Ky. 4½ x 3.

730 Grooved Axe, rough and irregular ; Breckenridge Co., Ky. 4 x 2½.

731 Rude grooved Axe, small ; Ky. 4 x 2.

732 Grooved Axe, the surface hardly changed from the condition in which it was found ; Breckenridge Co., Ky. 4 x 3.

733 Grooved Axe, reddish, resembles hematite, and like it is uncommonly dense ; Cooper Co., Mo. 5 x 4.

734 Grooved Axe, has been polished ; Breckenridge Co., Ky. 4 x 2½.

735 Grooved Axe, partially curved, head rounded ; Calhoun Co., Ill. 4½ x 3.

736 Grooved Axe, rounded, head flattened ; Breckenridge Co., Ky. 4½ x 3.

737 Grooved Axe of light stone, polished and finely made ; Huron Co., Ohio. 5 x 3.

738 Large grooved Axe of nearly black stone, surface nearly polished, end broken ; Massac Co., Ill. 7 x 5.

739 Grooved Axe of light granite, fine form ; Ill. 6 x 4.

740 Grooved Axe, nearly rectangular ; Ky. 6½ x 4.

741 Grooved Axe, head broken, partly polished ; Cooper Co., Mo. 6 x 3.

742 Grooved Axe, looks like diorite, groove broad and deep ; Beaver Co., Pa. 5½ x 3½.

743 Grooved Axe, resembles white marble, a rare material ; Franklin Co., Mo. 4½ x 3½.

744 Grooved Axe, small ; Breckenridge Co., Ky. 3½ x 3.

745 Grooved Axe of dark stone resembling diorite ; N. C. 4 x 3½.

746 Grooved Axe, slate ; Rhea Co., Tenn. 5 x 3½.

747 Grooved Axe, slate, of lighter color than the last ; E. Tenn. 5 x 4.

748 Grooved Axe, black slate ; Fond du Lac, Wis. 5 x 3½.

749 Grooved Axe, of dark, dense material ; N. C. 4½ x 3½.

750 Grooved Axe, finely made ; near Cowden, Mo. 4½ x 2½.

751　Grooved Axe of nice form, blue slate; Breckenridge Co., Ky. $4\frac{1}{2}$ x 3.

752　Grooved Axe, small size : Breckenridge Co., Ky.　4 x 2.

753　Grooved Axe, a white vein runs the entire length ; Rhea Co., Tenn.　5 x 3.

754　Grooved Axe, edge narrowed, head expanded ; Ky. $4x2\frac{1}{4}$.

755　Grooved Axe, nearly quadrangular, of slate ; E. Tenn. 5 x 5.

756　Grooved Axe of dark polished stone, like diorite ; Huron Co., Ohio.　5 x $2\frac{1}{2}$.

757　Grooved Axe of red sandstone, nearly oval ; Breckenridge Co., Ky. $5\frac{1}{2}$ x $3\frac{1}{2}$.

758　Grooved Axe of coarse reddish granite ; Ky.　4 x $2\frac{1}{2}$.

759　Grooved Axe, slate, partly polished ; Breckenridge Co., Ky. 4 x 2.

760　Grooved Axe, small, elongated, slate ; N. C.　$6\frac{1}{2}$ x $2\frac{1}{2}$.

761　Grooved Axe, bluish slate ; Ky.　$3\frac{1}{2}$ x 3.

762　Grooved Axe of reddish slate ; Breckenridge Co., Ky. 4 x 3.

763　Grooved Axe, somewhat irregular in form ; Breckenridge Co., Ky. $4\frac{1}{2}$ x $2\frac{1}{2}$.

764　Grooved Axe, has been smoothed and slightly polished, slate ; Breckenridge Co., Ky. $5\frac{1}{2}$ x $3\frac{1}{2}$.

765　Grooved Axe of slate, partly polished ; Breckenridge Co., Ky. 6 x 4.

766　Grooved Axe, of sharp grained sandstone ; Breckenridge Co., Ky. $5\frac{1}{2}$ x $3\frac{1}{2}$.

767　Grooved Axe, shows weathering where it has been broken ; Breckenridge Co., Ky.　5 x 4.

768　Large grooved Axe ; this is the largest I have ever met with, except one in the possession of Mrs. Maxwell, known as the " Colorado huntress," who exhibited a fine collection of American birds and animals at the Centennial in Philadelphia, 1876. Mrs. Maxwell died a victim to the ingratitude of the public. At her own expense she exhibited these animals and received not the slightest recognition of her exertions, not even a complimentary notice from the Government, to which she was fairly entitled, her exhibit being most creditable. This axe, owing to its large size, has been used as a Nut-stone, to crack black walnuts, to which use it is well adapted ; Cloverport, Breckenridge Co., Ky. Size 12 x $7\frac{1}{2}$ x 3.

769 Grooved Axe of light diorite; Breckenridge Co., Ky. 3½ x 2½.

CELTS.

The following Chisel-shaped objects, whether found in Europe or America, are generally denominated Celts. They are of various materials, of stone, iron, copper, bone, horn, etc.; many are beautifully polished, some are of jade and other rare materials, and are numbered from 770 to 948.

770 Celt of polished ribbon slate; very fine and rare; Tenn. River Flats, Rhea Co., Tenn. 11 x 3.

771 Celt of slate, partly polished, extra fine and rare; the largest and finest I have ever seen; Rhea Co., East Tenn. 14 x 2½.

772 Large Celt, polished all over, labeled "from Paris." 11 x 2½.

773 Celt, called a cutting celt, elegantly polished; Beaver Valley, Beaver Co., Pa. 9 x 2¾.

774 Fine Celt of dark slate, partly polished; Breckenridge Co., Ky. 10 x 4.

775 Celt of dark stone, resembles diorite, polished; Kingsbury, La Porte Co., Ind. 9 x 3.

776 Large handsome Celt, polished; Rhea Co., Tenn. 8½ x 3½.

777 Celt of black slate, round and polished all over; Rhea Co., Tenn. 7½ x 2¾.

778 Large oval Celt, various colors, partly white as though inlaid; Hancock Co., Ky. 6½ x 3.

779 Oval Celt, of light granite, polished; Mo. 6 x 3.

780 Celt of dark grained granite, nicely polished; Knox Co., Ohio. 6 x 2¾.

781 Celt, material like the last and as finely polished, square head; Franklin Co., Mo. 6 x 3.

782 Double bladed Celt, one point enlarged, polished, handsome and has fine cutting edge; Barton, Colbert Co., Ala. 6 x 2¾.

783 Celt of light colored polished granite, very fine; Knox Co., Tenn. 6 x 2½.

784 Celt of gray slate, edge a trifle chipped; Breckenridge Co., Ky. 7½ x 2½.

785 Celt of dark granite, polished, edges square; Cooper Co., Mo. 5 x 2½.

786 Celt of dark slate, edge broadly expanded; from same locality. 6½ x 4½.

787 Celt, nicely wrought, slate: N. Carolina. 5½ x 2.

788 Celt, finely finished; Lincoln Co., Tenn. 5 x 2.

789 Broad flat Celt, resembles light granite; Fairfield Co., S. C. 7½ x 4.

790 Celt, stone similar to the last, smooth, wrought nearly to a polish; S. Ill. 8 x 3½.

791 Celt of granite, expands towards the cutting point; Franklin Co., Mo. 7½ x 3.

792 Celt of dark granite, polished, extra fine; Hancock Co., Ky. 6 x 2½.

793 Celt of dark stone resembling slate, polished; labeled Lyon. 6 x 2½.

794 Celt, stone of several colors, one white in large portion; Montgomery Co., Miss. 6½ x 3½.

795 Celt of granite, expanded toward the end, polished; Franklin Co., Mo. 5½ x 3.

796 Celt of light colored granite; Montgomery Co., Miss. 5 x 3.

797 Celt of light colored slate, partly polished; Mason Co., W. Va. 5 x 3.

798 Celt of light gray granite, fine; Ill. 5 x 2½.

799 Celt of light sandstone, polished; Cooper Co., Mo. 6 x 2¾.

800 Small Celt, polished; Trumbull Co., Ohio. 3½ x 1½.

801 Celt of dark granite, polished; Beaver Co., Pa. 4 x 1¾.

802 Celt of nearly black stone, polished; Jefferson Co., N. Y. 3½ x 2.

803 Celt of green slate, partly polished; Massac Co., Ill. 4½ x 2½.

804 Celt of light colored stone, like granite; Franklin Co. Mo. 4 x 2.

805 Celt, looks like diorite, polished; Hog Island. 4½ x 2.

806 Small Celt of light granite; Cumberland River, Ky. 3½ x 2.

807 Cutting Celt, finished to be hafted; Beaver Co., Pa. 4 x 2.

808 Celt, nearly resembles diorite in its polish; Breckenridge Co., Ky. 5 x 2.

809 Celt of granite, polished; Cooper Co., Mo. 4 x 2.

810 Celt of slate; Indiana Co., Pa. 4 x 2.

811 Cutting Celt, shows secondary use as a hammer; Beaver Co., Pa. 4 x 2½.

812 Large, flat, double convex Celt, of granite; Carter, E.
Tenn. 8 x 4½.

813 Celt of grey granite, polished; Beaver Co., Pa. 6 x 3.

814 Celt of granite sprinkled with black, sides nearly parallel, polished; Pulaski Co., Ill. 7 x 3.

815 Dark oval Celt of granite; Cooper Co., Mo. 6 x 3.

816 Oval Celt of light colored granite, wrought to a cutting
edge, partly polished; Meade Co., Ky. 6½ x 3.

817 Oval Celt, well wrought, one side partly polished;
Macon Co., N. C. 5½ x 3.

818 Celt of black slate, polished; Huron Co., Ohio. 5½ x 2½.

819 Celt taken from a mound in second drift, Ohio Valley,
Pa. This Mound was constructed of boulders taken
from the surface and the contour completed with clay,
this interment not being coincident with origin. 6
x 3.

820 Celt of reddish sandstone, partly polished surface; Ky.
5⅓ x 2¼.

821 Celt, sides approaching parallel, granite; Michigan.
4½ x 2⅓.

822 Celt of sandstone, six sides, a rare form; Rideau Lake,
Westport, Ontario. 5⅓ x 2⅓.

823 Celt of diorite, beautifully mingled white and black;
Huron Co., Ohio. 4 x 2.

824 Small oval Celt, stone having a white vein; Vigo Co.,
Ind. 3½ x 2.

825 Celt, nearly triangular; Clay Co., Ky. 4 x 2½.

826 Celt of slate, nicely made; Beaver Co., Pa. 4½ x 2.

827 Celt, short, nearly quadrangular, polished; Jefferson
Co., N. Y. 3½ x 2.

828 Celt, top square, form nearly quadrangular, polished,
and has a cutting edge; Rhea Co., Tenn. 4½ x 2½.

829 Celt of fine granite, nearly square; Massac Co., Ill. 4
x 2.

830 Celt. of dark chocolate-colored granite, wrought to a
     cutting edge, polished ; Massac Co., Ill. $4\frac{1}{2}$ x $2\frac{1}{2}$.
831 Celt, slate, partly polished ; Breckenridge Co., Ky. 5
     x $2\frac{1}{2}$.
832 Long slender Celt, slate ; 'Rhea Co., Tenn. 8 x 2.
833 Celt, nearly quadrangular, granite ; Calhoun Co., Ill.
     $4\frac{1}{2}$ x 3.
834 Celt of similar material ; Indiana. $4\frac{1}{2}$ x $2\frac{1}{2}$.
835 Celt of dark material, flat on one side, polished surface ;
     Beaver Co., Pa. $4\frac{1}{2}$ x $2\frac{1}{2}$.
836 Celt of light granite ; Breckenridge Co., Ky. $4\frac{1}{2}$ x 2.
837 Celt, nearly quadrangular ; Houston Co., Tenn. 4 x $2\frac{1}{2}$.
838 Celt, sides nearly parallel, light granite or slate ; Rabun
     Co., Ga. $6\frac{1}{2}$ x 2.
839 Celt of coarse sandstone ; Meade Co., Ky. 5 x $2\frac{1}{2}$.
840 Celt of slate, partly polished ; Breckenridge Co., Ky.
     $4\frac{1}{2}$ x 2.
841 Cutting Celt of nearly black stone, intended for a han-
     dle ; Beaver Co., Pa. $4\frac{1}{2}$ x 2.
842 Cutting Celt ; Beaver Co., Pa. 6 x $2\frac{1}{4}$.
843 Long, slender Celt, appears to be adapted for a borer,
     for which it has evidently served in making perfora-
     tions. 8 x $1\frac{1}{4}$.
844 Small Celt ; Jones Cove, Sevier Co., Tenn. 5 x 2.
845 Small Celt, top pointed ; Breckenridge Co., Ky. $4\frac{1}{2}$x$2\frac{1}{2}$.
846 Celt of red sandstone ; Macon Co., N. C. 6 x $2\frac{1}{2}$.
847 Celt, partly polished ; Bone Island, Starke Co., Ind. $4\frac{1}{2}$
     x $2\frac{1}{2}$.
848 Celt, middle contracted ; Independence, Mo. $5\frac{1}{2}$ x $2\frac{1}{4}$.
849 Celt, end expanded ; Hot Spring Co., Ark. $4\frac{1}{2}$ x $2\frac{1}{2}$.
850 Celt of dark granite, has been polished ; Independence,
     Ark. 4 x $2\frac{1}{2}$.
851 Small handsome Celt ; Beaver Co., Pa. $3\frac{1}{2}$ x $1\frac{1}{2}$.
852 Small long Celt, with cutting edge at both ends ; Rhea
     Co., Tenn. 6 x $1\frac{1}{4}$.
853 Small narrow Celt with two cutting edges, polished ;
     Jackson Co., Ala. $3\frac{1}{2}$ x 1.
854 Celt, light stone. resembles novaculite, polished ; Todd
     Co., Ky. $3\frac{1}{2}$ x 3.
855 Small Celt of black slate ; Beaver Co., Pa. 3 x $1\frac{1}{2}$.

856 Small Celt of greenish slate; Beaver Co., Pa, 5 x 1½.
857 Small oval grey Celt; bank of the Ohio River. 3 x 2.
858 Celt of granite, sides nearly parallel; McKee's Rock, W. Pa. 7½ x 1½.
859 Celt, end enlarged, nicely polished; Carroll Co., Mo. 5 x 2½.
860 Celt, top nearly pointed, Chattooga River, Ga. 5½ x 2½.
861 Celt; Hot Spring Co., Ark. 6 x 2.
862 Celt of red stone ; from the same locality as No. 861. 4½ x 2½.
863 Celt of sandstone, partly polished ; Beaver Co., Pa. 5½ x 3½.
864 Celt of black and white stone, commingled ; Pike Co., Ill. 5 x 2½.
865 Celt of black slate ; Jefferson Co., N. Y. 4½ x 2.
866 Celt of blue slate, polished ; Macon Co., N. C. 4 x 2.
867 Celt of coarse stone ; Williamson Co., Ill. 4½ x 2.
868 Celt of slate, polished ; Rabun Co., Ga. 4 x 2.
869 Celt of slate, polished ; Meade Co., Ky. 4 x 2.
870 Small Celt of granite, one side polished. 4 x 1½.
871 Celt of reddish stone, polished ; Macon Co., N. C. 4 x 1½.
872 Celt Axe, polished ; Breckenridge Co., Ky. 4 x 2½.
873 Celt of black and white diorite; Ky. 3½ x 2.
874 Long, narrow, rounded Celt; Jackson Co., Ala. 6 x 1½.
875 Celt, patinated with a separate crust, which has largely peeled off. Marked by Mr. Spang "Curiosity"; fine ; Washington Co., Ohio. 6 x 2½.
876 Celt, slate ; Beaver Co., Pa. 5 x 2.
877 Celt of diorite ; Lincoln Co., Tenn. 4 x 2.
878 Celt of sandstone ; Clay Co., N. C. 5 x 2½.
879 Celt of slate ; Washington Co., Pa. 3½ x 2.
880 Narrow Celt of slate, polished. 5½ x 1½.
881 Rude Celt of slate; Beaver Co., Pa. 4 x 1½.
882 Celt, slate like diorite, polished ; Fairfield Co., S. C. 4 x 1½.
883 Celt of coarse stone ; Massac Co., Ill. 4 x 2.
884 Narrow Celt of slate, slightly gouge form ; Meigs Co., Tenn. 4 x 1.
885 Celt of slate, polished ; Beaver Co., Pa. 3½ x 1½.

886   Celt of slate, polished ; Mason Co., **W. Va.** $3\frac{1}{2}$ x 2.

887   Celt of green slate ; Pulaski Co., Ill. $3\frac{1}{2}$ x 2.

888   Celt of dark green stone, very fine ; Howell, Mo. $3\frac{1}{2}$
         x 2.   .

889   Celt of greenish veined slate ; Mason Co., Va.   4 x 2.

890   Small Celt; Vigo Co., Ind.   3 x $1\frac{1}{2}$.

891   Celt.   The buyer accused the finder of grinding it,
         which he denied ; Cooper Co., Mo.   3 x 2.

892   Small Celt ; Beaver Co., Pa. $2\frac{1}{2}$ x $1\frac{1}{2}$.

893   Celt of slate, rude ; Newyago Co., Mich.   4 x $2\frac{1}{3}$.

894   Celt of slate, polished ; Pulaski Co., Ill.   4 x 2.

895   Celt of slate, in form an irregular rhomboid ; Macon
         Co , N. C.   5 x $2\frac{1}{2}$.

896   Celt of clouded granite ; Ohio Valley, Pa. $3\frac{1}{2}$ x $1\frac{1}{2}$.

897   Celt, intended to be used with a handle ; Beaver Co.,
         Pa.   4 x 2.

898   Celt used with a handle, surface polished. $3\frac{1}{4}$ x $2\frac{1}{4}$.

899   Celt of slate ; Meade Co., Ky.   4 x 2.

900   Celt of chert, a material seldom used for the purpose ;
         S. Ill. $4\frac{1}{2}$ x 2.

901   Celt of variegated stone ; Rabun Co., N. Ga.   4 x $2\frac{1}{2}$.

902   Small Celt, mostly polished ; Mason Co., Va. $2\frac{1}{2}$ x $1\frac{1}{2}$.

903   Small black Celt, W. P. $2\frac{1}{3}$ x 2.

904   Small black Celt; Vigo Co., Ind.   3 x 2.

905   Small Celt, of chert or novaculite ; Clay Co., Ky. $2\frac{1}{2}$
         x 2.

906   Small Celt, Knox Co., E. Tenn. $2\frac{1}{2}$ x $1\frac{1}{2}$.

907   Small Celt, partly polished ; Beaver Co., Pa. $2\frac{1}{2}$ x $1\frac{1}{2}$.

908   Celt of black stone, said by Mr. Spang to be a " natural
         formation : " Beaver Co., Pa. $4\frac{1}{2}$ x 2.

909   Celt of rough material, probably granite ; Mo.   6 x 4.

910   Grooved Celt of slate : Rhea Co., Tenn. $4\frac{1}{2}$ x 2.

911   Small Celt ; Mason Co., Va. $1\frac{1}{2}$ x 1.

912   Small Celt, polished ; Beaver Co., Pa.   2 x 1.

913   Small Celt, polished ; Beaver Co., Pa.   2 x 1.

914   Small Celt, polished, end expanded ; Rhea Co., Tenn.
         3 x $1\frac{1}{3}$.

915   Celt of small composite stone, polished ; Hog Island.
         $2\frac{1}{2}$ x $1\frac{1}{2}$.

916 Celt of slate; Meade Co., Ky. $3\frac{1}{2}$ x 2.
917 Celt of purple slate, polished; Rhea Co., Tenn. $3\frac{1}{2}$ x $1\frac{1}{2}$.
918 Fleshing Celt, green slate, polished; Beaver Co., Pa. $3\frac{1}{2}$ x $1\frac{1}{2}$.
919 Celt, with fine cutting edge; polished; Massac Co., Ill. 4 x 2.
920 Celt of slate; Rabun Co., Ga. 4 x 2.
921 Celt of black slate, polished. 3 x $1\frac{1}{2}$.
922 Celt of slate; Ohio Valley, Beaver Co., Pa. 4 x $1\frac{1}{2}$.
923 Celt, small but fine; Independence, Mo. $3\frac{1}{2}$ x 2.
924 Celt of light composite stone, in which white predominates; Montgomery Co., Ark.
925 Celt of dark slate, nearly polished; Sevier Co., Tenn. $3\frac{1}{2}$ x $1\frac{1}{2}$.
926 Celt of light slate, seems to be a natural formation, neatly wrought; Cumberland Co., Ky. $3\frac{1}{2}$ x 2.
927 Small Celt of slate; Montgomery Co., Ark. $2\frac{1}{2}$ x 1.
928 Small Celt of dark polished slate; Rhea Co., E. Tenn. 3 x $1\frac{1}{2}$.
929 Small Celt of novaculite; Massac Co., Ill. 3 x $1\frac{1}{2}$.
930 Small Celt of diorite, black and white mingled, polished; Beaver Co., Pa. $3\frac{1}{2}$ x 2.
931 Celt of reddish granite, partly polished; Swaine Co., N. C. 3 x 1.
932 Celt of diorite, edge slightly chipped; Beaver Co., Pa. 4 x 2.
933 Celt of nearly black slate, cutting edge; Breckenridge Co., Ky. 3 x 2.
934 A rubbing or burnishing Celt; Beaver Co., Pa. $2\frac{1}{2}$x$1\frac{1}{2}$.
935 Dark Celt, probably a rubbing celt; Lincoln Co., Tenn. $2\frac{1}{2}$ x 2.
936 Large Celt, broken, surface polished; Beaver Co., Pa. 4 x $2\frac{1}{2}$.
937 Celt of light sandstone; Lincoln Co., Tenn. 4 x $2\frac{1}{2}$.
938 Celt of jade from Australia, one of the finest objects in the sale, cost in Paris 80 francs, elegantly polished; 7 $\frac{1}{2}$x $4\frac{1}{2}$.
939 Flint Celt from Scandinavia. This beautiful axe or celt is made by the process usually called carving, and is a splendid example of that work. $11\frac{1}{2}$ x 3.

940 Ungrooved Axe from Scandinavia, flint, polished on both its flats and edges ; very fine and rare. 6 x 3.

941 Celt, flats and edges all polished, flint, Scandinavia. 5½ x 2¾.

942 Flint Celt, flats and edges all polished, bought in Paris ; Scandinavia. 6 ½ x 2½.

943 Flint Celt, finished all over by the process of chipping, called carving ; Scandinavia. 5 x 2½.

944 Hollow Celt or gouge, an article appropriately named by European Archaeologists as a hollow axe, polished inside and out, and finely finished ; Scandinavia. 6½ x 2.

945 Hollow Celt or gouge, of the kind almost peculiar to New England ; dark, nearly black slate ; Ottey Lake, near Perth, Ontario, Canada.. 6 x 2.

946 Gouge of slate, nicely finished ; Madison Co., N. Y. 5 x 1½.

947 Gouge of light stone, well formed ; Jo. Davies Co., Ill. 3½ x 1½.

948 Gouge of purple slate ; Oneida Co., N. Y. 4½ x 1½.

949 · Paleolithic implement, resembles a cold chisel ; from Perigueux (Dordogne), France. 6 x 2.

950 Hematite Celt ; Lodi, Montgomery Co., Miss. 3¼ x 1¼.

PESTLES.

Cylindrical, and other forms.

951 Long cylindrical Pestle, veined or clouded with white ; Long Island, Holstein River, E. Tenn. 18½ x 2½.

952 Cylindrical Pestle of slate, one end nearly celt-shaped ; Rhea Co., Tenn. 15½ x 2.

953 Long cylindrical Pestle of granite, roughly finished, though of good form. 16½ x 2½.

954 Cylindrical Pestle of slate, nearly square ; Oneida Co., N. Y. 14½ x 2½.

955 Cylindrical Pestle of dark granite ; Macon Co., N. C. 11½ x 2.

956 Rough round Pestle, end celt-form, large end nearly polished ; Rhea Co., Tenn. 11½ x 3.

957 Long round Pestle of slate ; Rabun Co., Ga. 12 x 2.

958 Long Pestle of purple slate, approaching the square
form. $10\frac{1}{2}$ x 2.

959 Long Pestle of slate, flattened : Breckenridge Co., Ky.
12 x $8\frac{1}{2}$.

960 Short thick Pestle of slate. $9\frac{1}{2}$ x $2\frac{1}{2}$.

961 Cylindrical Pestle of slate, enlarged in the middle ;
Ohio. $9\frac{1}{2}$ x $2\frac{1}{2}$.

962 Cylindrical Pestle of dark granite ; Oneida Co., N. Y.
$7\frac{1}{2}$ x $2\frac{1}{2}$.

963 Cylindrical Pestle of dark slate ; Beaver Co., Pa. $7\frac{1}{2}$
x 3.

964 Round Pestle of sandstone; Beaver Co., Pa. $8\frac{1}{2}$ x 2.

965 Small round Pestle, cylindrical ; Fairfield Co., S. C. 8
x 2.

966 Short round Pestle of blue slate; Breckenridge Co.,
Ky. 8 x $2\frac{1}{2}$.

967 Round Pestle of mica slate ; Rabun Co., Ga. 7 x 2.

968 Small round Pestle of mica slate. 6 x 2.

969 Cylindrical Pestle, approaches conical ; Hot Spring Co.,
Ark. $5\frac{1}{2}$ x 3.

970 Cylindrical Pestle, end enlarged ; Rhea Co., Tenn. $6\frac{1}{2}$
x 3.

971 Round Pestle, with handle, of mushroom shape. $5\frac{1}{2}$
x $3\frac{1}{2}$.

972 Round Pestle, one extremity more enlarged than the
other, with hollow depression ; sandstone ; Meade
Co., Ky. $5\frac{1}{2}$ x $3\frac{1}{2}$.

973 Pestle, mushroom shape, approaching conical form, to
be grasped by the hand, apparently for cracking
nuts; red sandstone ; Hancock Co., Ky. $5\frac{1}{2}$ x $3\frac{1}{2}$.

974 Conical Pestle, mushroom shape ; Clay Co., Ky. 5
x $3\frac{1}{2}$.

975 Conical Pestle or nut-cracker ; Lincoln Co., Tenn. 4
x 3.

976 Conical Pestle of coarse granite ; Pulaski Co., Ill. 5
x 3.

977 Conical Pestle for cracking nuts ; Breckenridge Co.,
Ky. 5 x $3\frac{1}{2}$.

978 Conical Pestle of black diorite, handle with an enlarged
top, fine. 4 x 3.

979   Conical Pestle of coarse sandstone ; Meade Co., Ky.   4
        x 3.
980   Conical Pestle, stone light, nearly white ; Ky.   5 x 3.
981   Conical Pestle, much worn ; Breckenridge Co., Ky.   4
        x 2½.
982   Conical Pestle ; Hancock Co., Ky.   3½ x 3.
983   Conical Pestle ; Breckenridge Co., Ky.   3½ x 3.

NUT STONES.

These stones are very common throughout the western country. Most
of them are made with several depressions, evidently produced for cracking nuts.

984   Nut stone or anvil.   Mr. Spang notes the difference
        between this and the usual form found throughout
        the Ohio Valley. This anvil has conical depressions
        while concavities of the usual nut stones are more
        basin or cup shape. Sandstone having ten concavi-
        ties.   Cooper Co., Mo.   5½ x 4.
985   Nut stone, with two large concavities ; Ohio Valley.   8
        x 7.
986   Anvil stone with but one large depression ; Allegheny
        Co., Pa.   7 x 5.
987   Anvil stone with three very large and deep depressions ;
        Allegheny Co., Pa.   11 x 6½.
988   Anvil or nut stone, sandstone with four depressions ;
        Allegheny Co., Pa.   9 x 7.
989   Small Nut stone, five depressions.   5 x 3½.
990   Large Maul or hammer, used in prehistoric copper min-
        ing at Lake Superior ; Isle Royale, L. S.   7 x 6½.
991   Maul or sledge hammer, from the same region and has
        evidently been used for ages.   4½ x 4½.
992   Maul or hammer ; Pawnee Co., Kan.   4 x 3¼.
993   Grooved Hammer or maul of granite.   3¼ x 3¼.
994   Grooved Hammer or maul ; Clay Co., N. C.   5½ x 3.
995   Flaking Hammer, Allegheny River, Pa.   4 x 3.
996   Conical flaking Hammer, of quartzite ; Macon Co., N.
        C.   3½ x 3.
997   Hammer stone of quartzite ; Swaine Co., N. C.   2¼ x 2¼.
987a Large Mortar of stone ; the inside and outside are cov-
        ered with perforations extending part way through
        the object ; a curious and fine vessel.   10 x 7.

998 Pottery Pestle from beside a mound; Rhea Co., Tenn.
     Adapted for the mortar No. 997a. 7 x 4.
999 Shallow vessel of potstone ; a mortar. 9 x 6½.
1000 Stone Mortar, shallow depression ; Black Hawk, Mo.
     7½ x 6.
1001 Nearly cubical formed stone, has at opposite sides two
     depressions for the fingers. Its use is unknown, but
     may have been used for casting or throwing, after the
     manner of quoits ; an unique object; size 6 x 5 x 5.

HAMMER STONES.

1002 Grooved Hammer Stone, quadrangular ; Ohio. 4 x 3.
1003 Grooved Hammer Stone, nearly oval ; Hebron, Ind.
     4 x 3.
1004 Hammer Stone, has four depressions, coarse sandstone,
     very rare form ; Washington Co., Ark. 4½ x 2½.
1005 Hammer Stone, with two depressions, of reddish gran-
     ite ; Yadkin River, Montgomery Co., N. C. 4 x 2¼.
1006 Water worn Hammer stone, grooved all round ; Phil-
     lips Co., Kan. 5 x 4.
1007 Hammer stone with two depressions ; Tarentum, Pa.
     4 x 3.
1008 Hammer stone with two opposite depressions, of sand-
     stone ; Hot Springs, Ark. 4½ x 3.
1009 Oval Anvil or hammer stone, two depressions ; Pulas-
     ki Co., Ill. 3 x 2.
1010 Anvil stone, two depressions ; Montgomery, Ala. 3
     x 2½.
1011 Hammer stone, water worn ; fine. 3 x 2.
1012 Anvil stone, oval ; Black Hawk, Mo. 4½ x 4.
1013 Grooved Hammer stone, light granite, oval, well
     wrought ; West. No. Carolina. 4 x 2¾.
1014 Anvil stone, kidney shape, of quartzite ; Yadkin River,
     N. C. 4 x 2¾.
1015 Grooved Hammer stone, of quartzite, nicely wrought ;
     Shelby Co., Ohio. 2¾ x 2.
1016 Grooved Hammer stone ; Seneca Co., Ohio. 3 x 2.
1017 Grooved Hammer stone, kidney shape and color, nicely
     finished ; Peoria Co., Ill. 4½ x 3.
1018 Hammer stone, probably a flaking hammer ; Lincoln
     Co., Tenn. 3 x 3.

1019   Hammer stone with four depressions; M. Tenn. $3\frac{1}{2}$x2.

1020   Hammer stone with depressions; Lincoln Co., Tenn. 4 x 3.

1021   Hammer stone with depressions; Yadkin River, N. C. 5 x 3.

1022   Hammer stone, two large deep depressions; Yadkin River, N. C. $3\frac{1}{2}$ x 3.

1023   Hammer stone, two opposite depressions; Cooper Co., 4 x 3.

1024   Hammer stone, similar to last but of light stone ; Lincoln Co., Tenn. 4 x 3.

1025   Hammer stone, two depressions, of quartzite; Yadkin River, N. C. 3 x 3.

1026   Stone Ball or hammer stone ; Beaver Co., Pa. 3 x 3.

1027   Large stone Ball or hammer stone; Beaver Co., Pa. $3\frac{1}{2}$ x $3\frac{1}{2}$.

1028   Hammer stone, of dark material; West. N. C. 4 x 3.

1029   Hammer stone or ball, shows signs of use. 2 x $2\frac{1}{2}$.

1030   Stone Hammer, oval, water worn ; West. N. C. 4 x 3.

1031   Hammer or chipping stone ; West. Pa. $4\frac{1}{2}$ x 3.

1032   Hammer stone or ball; Beaver Co., Pa. 3 x 3.

1033   Chipping stone of ferruginous stone : Yadkin River, N. C. 3 x 3.

1034   Flaking hammer ; Allegheny Co., Pa. 3 x $2\frac{1}{2}$.

1035   Flaking hammer ; Allegheny Co., Pa. 3 x 3.

1036   Flaking hammer, shows evident signs of much use; Southwestern N. C. 6 x $4\frac{1}{2}$.

1037   Flaking hammers, Montgomery Co., Ala. 4 x 3.

1038   Flaking hammer ; Montgomery Co., Ala. 4 x 3.

1039   Flaking hammer ; Decatur, Ala. $2\frac{1}{2}$ x $1\frac{1}{2}$.

1040   Flaking hammer ; same locality. 3 x 2.

1041   Flaking hammer ; Decatur, Ala. $2\frac{1}{2}$ x 2.

1042   Another, from the same locality. $2\frac{1}{2}$ x 2.

GREAT SPADES.

The edges of most of these Spades are polished by long continued use, probably in mound building. They are of different material, comprising feldspar, chert, etc.

1043   Great Spade, edge finely polished, one of the largest I have ever seen ; Marion Co., Ill. 14 x 5.

1044   Great Spade, the edge seems to be of different material from the other portion, and appears to be of red jasper, polished on the sides and edges, partly including the red portion ; Pulaski Co., Ill. 10½ x 4.

1045   Great Spade, end polished on both sides; Pulaski Co., Ill. 12 x 4½.

1046   Great Spade, end polished, very fine ; Caledonia, Ill. 9 x 4½.

1047   Great Spade, end polished, fine and rare ; Massac Co., 11 x 4.

1048   Great Spade, end polished ; Mound, Massac Co., Ill. 11 x 4.

1049   Large Spade or shovel, edge polished ; Caledonia, Ill. 9½ x 5.

1050   Large Hoe or spade, end polished ; Pulaski Co., Ill. 7½ x 6.

1051   Large Spade of chert or sandstone, rounded at the end ; Ill. 8 x 7.

1052   Disc shaped Spade, partly polished ; Massac Co., Ill. 5½ x 5.

1053   Great Spade, polished over a large portion of it ; without doubt used in mound building ; Wayne Co., Ill.

1054   Nearly triangular Spade, chert; Massac Co., Ill. 8½ x 6.

1055   Great Spade of chert; from a mound, Massac Co., Ill. 7½ x 4.

1056   Great Spade, end polished by long use ; Pulaski Co., Ill. 10½ x 3½.

1057   Great Spade, partly polished ; same locality. 9½ x 4½.

1058   Great Spade, largely polished ; Massac Co., Ill. 9 x 4.

1059   Great Spade, partly polished with special elegance ; Clinton Co., Ill. 9 x 4.

1060   Great Spade, end polished ; Pulaski Co., Ill. 9 x 4.

1061   Great Spade, of dark colored chert, end polished in its entire breadth, and finely done. Marion Co., Ky. 10 x 5.

1062   Great Spade, nearly oval ; Cloverport, Ky. 9 x 6.

1063   Great Spade, surface patinated with different colors ; Olmstead, Ill. 13 x 4½.

1064   Great Spade, surface polished ; from a mound, Massac Co., Ill. 14 x 5.

1065 Great Spade, surface polished toward the end ; from a mound in the same locality. $9\frac{1}{3}$ x 4.

1066 Great Spade, polished on one end; Caledonia, Ill. 9 x $4\frac{1}{4}$.

1067 Great Spade, the outer and inner coating polished at the end ; from a mound, Massac Co., Ill. 9 x $4\frac{1}{2}$.

1068 Great Spade of chert, polished near the end; same locality. $10\frac{1}{4}$ x $3\frac{1}{2}$.

1069 Paddle-shaped Spade, near the end polished in the greater part of its breadth ; Caledonia, Ill. 10 x $5\frac{1}{2}$.

1070 Spade, partly polished ; from the same place. 8 x 5.

1071 Another large Spade, of uncommon thickness; from the same location. $8\frac{1}{8}$ x 4.

1072 Great Spade, end without polish but one of the flats partly so; Grand Chain, Ill. 11 x $4\frac{1}{2}$.

1073 Great Spade, one end slightly polished ; Caledonia, Ill. 10 x 4.

1074 Disc-shaped Hoe, or implement of agriculture ; about 250 of these objects were found in one pile, fine ; E. St. Louis, Mo.

1075 Leaf-shaped Spade, appears to be feldspar, fine ; Jackson Co., Mo.

1076 Great Spade, end polished ; Pulaski Co., Ill. $10\frac{1}{2}$x$3\frac{1}{2}$.

1077 Large Spade of dark stone, probably chert, end finely polished ; Massac Co., Ill. 8 x 4.

1078 Large Spade, end polished, of the same material as the last ; from a mound in the same region. 8 x 4.

1078a Large Spade, same material as 1078, the end has a fine polish ; Todd Co., Ky. $8\frac{1}{2}$ x 3.

1079 Large disc-shaped 'Hoe of chert, edges notched, fine ; Massac Co., Ill. $5\frac{1}{2}$ x 4.

1080 Large Spade or celt, of dark chert, end polished ; Pulaski Co., Ill. 7 x 3.

1081 Large Spade, appears to be feldspar; Franklin Co., Mo. 7 x $3\frac{1}{2}$.

1082 Large Spade, the interior has a bluish cast ; New Palestine, Mo. $6\frac{1}{2}$ x 4.

1083 Large Spade of light stone ; Pulaski Co., Ill. 8 x $3\frac{1}{4}$.

1084 Large Spade of chert ; same locality. $8\frac{1}{2}$ x 3.

1085 Large Spade ; Cooper Co., Mo. 7 x $2\frac{1}{2}$.

1086 Large Spade, surface patinated ; Pulaski Co., Ill. 7x3.

1087   Large Spade, in form nearly elliptical, of light sharp-grained sandstone. 8½ x 3.

1088   Spade of dark chert; Cumberland Co., Ky. 6 x 3.

1089   Large Spade, variegated stone of handsome colors, end polished; Cooper Co., Mo. 6½ x 3.

1090   Imperfect disc-shaped Hoe, end polished; Pulaski Co., Ill. 5 x 5.

1091   Large Hoe, in form nearly rectangular; Cooper Co., Mo. 6½ x 2½.

1092   Large Spade of chert, end polished; Cumberland Co., Ky. 7½ x 3.

1093   Nearly round Hoe, edges notched, Massac Co., Ill. 5 x 4½.

1094   Large Spade of white stone; Cooper Co., Mo. 8½ x 4.

1095   Large Spade of white stone, surface patinated on both sides; Pulaski Co., Ill. 8½ x 3½.

1096   Large Spade of sandstone; Lincoln Co., Tenn. 7x2½.

1097   Large Spade; Missouri. 6½ x 2½.

1098   Large disc-shaped Hoe, has hollow base and notched edges; Sandy Ridge, Ill. 5 x 4½.

1099   Spade of chert, variegated and handsome; Lincoln Co., Tenn.

1100   Spade, sides nearly parallel, very fine: Barton, Ala.

1101   Spade, sides nearly parallel, end polished; Cooper Co., Mo. 5½ x 1½.

1102   Spade of light blue stone, fine; Montgomery Co., Ark. 5 x 2.

1103   Spade; Cooper Co., Mo. 6½ x 2½.

1104   Spade of chert; Barton, Ala, 6 x 2.

1105   Spade; Colbert Co., Ala. 7 x 2½.

1106   Spade, sides nearly parallel; Massac Co., Ill. 7½ x 2.

1107   Spade of yellow chert, sides parallel, partly polished; Barton, Ala. 7 x 2.

1108   Spade, one end polished, Williamson Co., Ill. 6½ x 3.

1109   Elliptical Spade, one side polished, fine; Jersey Co., Ill. 7 x 2½.

1110   Long Spade; Missouri. 8 x 2.

1111   Spade, form approaching oval; Pulaski Co., Ill. 6 x 3.

1112   Spade of light stone, both sides near the end elegantly polished; Mo. 7½ x 3½.

1113 Large white colored Spade, unpolished; Barton, Ala.
      9 x 2½.

1114 Spade of irregular form; Franklin Co., Mo.   6½
      x 3.

1115 Spade, in part polished; Barton, Ala.   5 x 4.

1116 Spade of dark chert, partly polished; Massac Co., Ill.
      5½ x 2½.

1117 Spade of nearly white stone, end polished with use;
      Cooper Co., Mo.

1118 Elliptical Spade of reddish stone; Pulaski Co., Ill.
      5½ x 2½.

1119 Spade, bears the marks of ancient patination; Cooper
      Co., Mo.   5½ x 2.

1120 Spade, sides nearly parallel, of pink-colored chert partly
      polished; same locality.   7½ x 2.

1121 Broad elliptical Spade; from the same locality as the
      last.   5½ x 2½.

1122 Small Spade, one end partly polished; Cooper Co.,
      Mo.   5 x 2.

1123 Small Spade, end partly polished; Barton, Ala.   5
      x 2½.

1124 Gouge Celt of chert; Barton, Ala.   4½ x 2½.

1125 Small Spade; Pulaski Co., Ill.   4 x 2.

1126 Small Spade, Cooper Co., Mo.   5½ x 2.

1127 Small Spade, shows great wear, one end polished;
      Chariton Co., Mo.   5 x 2.

1128 Small Spade; from same locality.   3½ x 2.

1129 Small Spade; Independence, Mo.   4 x 2.

1130 Small Spade of feldspar of handsome color. This was
      plowed up with 44 others all alike, and found in a
      cache, Kingsbury, Ind.   Numbers 1130 to 1138 are a
      part of this find.   4 x 2½.

1131 Small Spade, a duplicate of the last but more pro-
      nounced in color; fine.   4 x 2½.

1132 Another, equally fine.

1133—38 Duplicates, all fine.   6 pcs.

1139 Spade of feldspar, a very fine object, received from Mr.
      Noe of Indianapolis; surface find, Floyd Co., Ind.
      6 x 2½.

UNFINISHED WORK.

Amongst the objects classed as "unfinished," a large number may be found, running from Amulets to Spear Heads, etc., many of them are very interesting and worthy of note, comprising Banner Stones, Amulets, Pipes, and many other forms, some amongst the most interesting of these objects.

1140 Pipe, blocked out, not perforated, fine ; Beaver Co., Pa. 4 x 2.

1141 Pipe or tube, partly perforated ; Lewis Co., Ky. 5½x2.

1142 Partly perforated Tube ; Defiance Co., Ohio. 4 x 2.

1143 Pipe or tube, partly perforated, very fine and neat perforation ; Shelby Co., Ohio. 3½ x 1½.

1144 Pipe or tube, nicely finished, perforation very neat but unfinished ; Ohio. 4½ x 1¼.

1145 Tube, partly perforated ; Fulton Co., Ohio. 4 x 1½.

1146 Tube for a pipe, partly bored ; Fulton Co., Ohio. 3¼ x 1¼.

1147 Nearly square, partly perforated, Tube ; Fulton Co., Ohio. 5 x 1.

1148 Large Tube, perforated throughout ; Licking Co., Ohio. 5 x 2.

1149 Large perforated Tube, one end narrowed, perhaps a natural formation ; Licking Co., Ohio. 4 x 2.

1150 Tube, perforation commenced, resembles graphite granite ; Breckenridge Co., Ky. 2 x 2.

1151 Unfinished object of Quartzite, has been used as a rubbing stone ; Ky. 3 x 2.

1152 Unfinished object, resembles No. 1150 in form, no perforation ; Breckenridge Co., Ky. 3½ x 3.

1153 Triangular stone, perforation commenced ; North Carolina. 3 x 2½.

1154 Triangular stone, dark, heavy granite ; Ky. 2½ x 2.

1155 Pipe of pink quartzite, perforation commenced ; Swaine Co., N. C. 3 x 2.

1156 Neat perforated stone, at the bottom of which is a nipple ; Ky. 2½ x 1¼.

1157 Needle of slate for sewing reindeer skins, surface polished ; Massac Co., Ill. 6 x 1.

1158 Oval Banner Stone, partly perforated and polished ; Martin Co., Ky. 4 x 1½.

1159 Imperfect Gorget; Shelby Co., Ohio. $3\frac{1}{2}$ x 2.

1160 Banner Stone, broken across the perforation, otherwise fine; Massac Co., Ill. 3 x 1.

1161 Banner Stone, perforation commenced ; Breckenridge Co., Ky. $3\frac{1}{4}$ x $1\frac{1}{2}$.

1162 Gorget, two perforations, rude ; Seneca Co., Ohio. 4 x $1\frac{1}{2}$.

1163 Imperfect Gorget without perforations; Rhea Co., Tenn. 4 x $2\frac{1}{2}$.

1164 Banner Stone, large perforation commenced ; James Co., Tenn. $4\frac{1}{2}$ x $1\frac{1}{2}$.

1165 Imperfect Banner Stone ; Kentucky. $4\frac{1}{2}$ x $1\frac{1}{2}$.

1166 Imperfect Banner Stone, partly finished ; Yadkin River, N. C. 4 x $2\frac{1}{2}$.

1167 Imperfect Banner Stone of curiously marked ribbon slate ; Williams Co., Ohio. 5 x 2.

1168 Small Banner Stone, perforation commenced ; Breckenridge Co., Ky. 2 x $1\frac{1}{2}$.

1169 Mica slate Pendant, two perforations commenced ; Ga. $3\frac{1}{2}$ x $2\frac{1}{4}$.

1170 Rhomb-spar object, perforation begun ; a pretty article ; Massac Co., Ill. $1\frac{1}{4}$ x $1\frac{1}{4}$.

1171 Iron ore object, perforation commenced ; Yadkin River, N. C. 2 x $1\frac{1}{2}$.

1172 Banner Stone with large perforation, slate; Rabun Co., Ga. $5\frac{1}{2}$ x $2\frac{1}{2}$.

1173 Perforated object, perforation gradually contracted toward the centre ; Ga. 6 x 2.

1174 Amulet of dark stone, bifurcated in form, blocked out but not polished ; Blackford Co., Ind. 10 x $2\frac{1}{4}$.

1175 Amulet, shaped liked the last, slate, irregularly finished ; Wyandotte Co., Ohio.

1176 Banner Stone of ribbon slate, imperforate ; Lake Shore, Ohio. $6\frac{1}{2}$ x 3.

1177 Banner Stone, also of ribbon slate, imperforate ; Miami Co., Ind. 5 x $2\frac{1}{2}$.

1178 Banner Stone, an unfinished object ; Shelby Co., Ohio. 6 x 3.

1179 Banner Stone, butterfly-shaped, of ribbon slate, unfinished and imperforate ; N. C. 5 x $3\frac{1}{2}$.

1180 Banner Stone of purple slate, imperforate; Massac Co., Ill. 3¼ x 3¼.
1181 Winder of slate, banner form ; Logan Co., Ohio. 7½x5.
1182 Banner Stone, imperforate ; Hardin Co., Ohio. 4½ x*3.
1183 Banner Stone, imperfect. 3 x 2¼.
1184 Paint Stone, red ; in form a pendant ; Independence, Mo. 4 x 1½.
1185 Partly finished object of iron ore ; Shelby Co., Ohio. 3 x 3.
1186 Object similar to the last in form ; Marion Co., Ohio.
1187 Stone Strigil or skin scratcher ; Beaver Co., Pa. 5½x2¼.
1188 Another similar object ; Yadkin Co., N. C. 4 x 3.
1189 Another Strigil ; Beaver Co., Pa. 6½ x 3.
1190 Sandstone Strigil ; same location. 5¼ x 3.
1191 Another similar object ; Rochester, Pa. 4½ x 1¼.
1192 Another of same description ; Beaver Co., Pa. 3½x1½.
1193 Another. 3¼ x 2.
1194 Another, of quartzite ; Montgomery Co., Ala. 3 x 2.

STONE BEADS, ETC., ETC.

1195 Bead of agate, prettily marked and handsomely polished, very fine, of large size. These beads are rare and beautiful ; the color is of robin's egg blue ; N. C. ¾ x ¾.
1196 Another agate Bead, prettier than the last ; N. C. 1x¾.
1197 Bead of agate or chalcedony, but smaller ; same locality.
1198 Perforated black stone Bead, fine ; dia. ¾ inch.
1199 Perforated Beads of green stone, fine. 3 pcs., each ⅓ inch dia.
1200 Perforated Bead of dark green slate, very fine and rare ; N. Carolina. ½ in. dia.
1201 Agate Bead of smaller size than No. 1196, beautifully marked and polished ; N. Carolina. ¾ in. long.
1202 Perforated Bead of blue stone, fine and rare. ¼ in. dia.
1203 Perforated flat Bead of sandstone ; N. C. 1 in. dia.
1204 Perforated Beads of bone and stone, fine ; N. Carolina and Ky. 4 pcs.
1205 Perforated Bead of black stone, resembling hematite ; N. Carolina. ¾ in. dia.

1206 Perforated flat Bead of slate ; N. Carolina. 1 in. dia.

1207 Another flat Bead, uncommon and rare. N. Carolina. 1 in. diameter.

1208 Long perforated Bead of silicious stone, which appears to be a compact iron ore; Lodi, Miss. $1\frac{1}{3}$ x $\frac{3}{4}$.

1209 Perforated Bead of bone, groove all around, fine; Tenn. $\frac{1}{2}$ in. dia.

1210 Perforated pottery Beads longitudinally pierced, fine and rare. 2 pcs.

1211 Large perforated Bead of slate, fine, and rare when of this size; N. C. $1\frac{1}{2}$ x $\frac{5}{8}$.

1212 Large perforated Bead, the orifice large ; N. C. 1 x $\frac{3}{4}$.

1213 Perforated stone Beads, several broken, still fine. 4 pcs.

1214 Perforated flat stone Bead ; N. Carolina. $\frac{3}{4}$ in. dia.

1215 Thick round stone Bead with large perforation ; M. Tenn. $\frac{3}{4}$ in. dia.

1216 Perforated stone Pendant, a pretty stone, nicely carved ; Cherokee Co., N. C. $1\frac{1}{2}$ x $\frac{3}{4}$.

1217. Octagonal stone Bead, perforated near one corner, polished and very fine; same locality. $1\frac{1}{4}$ x $1\frac{1}{4}$.

1218 A small Celt, beautifully polished and rare; N. Carolina. 1 x $\frac{1}{2}$.

1219 Small heart-shaped pendant, with three holes. Concerning this pendant Mr. Spang treats us to an amusing account of his agent's attempt to open the mound in which this object was found ; Cloverport, Ky. $1\frac{1}{2}$ x 1.

1220 Small Gorget with one perforation, very rare when so tiny ; Oneida Co., N. Y. 2 x $1\frac{1}{2}$.

1221 An Amulet; this object reminds us at once of a burro with a pack on his back, and appears to be of modern Indian work. It is striking and peculiar ; Macon Co., N. C. $1\frac{3}{4}$ x $1\frac{1}{2}$.

1222 Perforated Banner Stone or celt, polished, of slate, rare in both form and material, a perforated celt being a rarity ; Swaine Co., N. C. 3 x $1\frac{1}{2}$.

1223 Perforated Pendant, polished, countersunk on both sides ; Ky. $4\frac{1}{2}$ x 3.

1224 Grooved Celt with three longitudinal grooves, fine and rare ; Missouri. 4 x $2\frac{1}{2}$.

1225 Imperfect Gorget with three holes; Lincoln Co., Tenn. 2 x 2.

1226 Gorget, half-shield-shape, broken at the perforation ; Peoria Co., Ill. 3 x 3.

1227 Gorget of alabaster, or sulphate of barytes, fine and rare ; Barton, Ala. 1½ x 1¼.

1228 Pendant or tally stone, the ends marked with numerous tallies, scarce ; Fairfield Co., S. C. 1½ x 1.

1229 Gorgets ; Allegheny Co., Pa. 2 x 1. 2 pcs.

1230 Gorget, four small perforations ; another single one ; Tenn. and Ohio. 2 x ½. 2 pcs.

1231 Gorget, or pierced tablet, of ribbon slate, polished ; Delaware Co., Ohio. 4 x 2.

1232 Gorget, several small perforations; another smaller one ; Missouri and So. Carolina. 2 pcs.

1233 Banner-stone, two perforations ; Pendant, broken at the perforation ; N. Y. and Ohio. 2 pcs.

1234 Gorgets, two pieces ; one has two, the other one, perforation. Pa. and Ala.

1235 Slender Celt, slate ; Montgomery Co., Ark. 5 x 1.

1236 Small Celt of slate ; North Carolina. 2¼ x 1.

1237 Short, narrow Celt, polished ; Meigs Co., Tenn. 3 x 1.

1238 Celt, double pointed, fine and small ; Macon Co., N.C. 3 x ¾.

1239 Narrow Celt of slate ; same locality. 3 x ¾.

1240 Narrow Celt of slate, fine ; Rhea Co., Tenn. 3½ x ¾.

1241 Gouge or celt, one flat hollowed, fine so small ; Oneida Co., N. Y. 1¾ x ¾.

1242 Celt of slate, narrow cutting edge ; Mason Co., Va. 2 x 1.

1243 Broad Celt, with cutting edge, polished ; Missouri. 2½ x 1¼.

1244 Broad Celt, nearly triangular ; Huron Co., Ohio. 2½x1½.

1245 Stone Burnisher, used for polishing raw hides, ends notched. 3 x 1.

1246 Canoe-shaped object ; near Greenwich, Ohio. 2½ x 1.

1247 Burnisher or rubbing stone, of dark slate ; Oneida Co., N. Y. 2 x 1½.

1248 Rare implement, of uncertain use ; McKee's Rock, Allegheny Co., Pa. 3 x 1½.

1249   Stone Needle used for sewing skins. 4 x 1.
1250   Tally Stone, each side with two notches; North Carolina. 2½ x 1.
1251   Marking Stone, has two perforations marked with deeply incised lines; Madison Co., N. Y. 2 x 1.
1252   Banner Stone, nearly oval, perforation commenced; N. C. 2 x 1½.
1253   Rubbing Stone of hematite; from same locality. 2x1.
1254   Pendant of curious shape, nearly round, fine and rare; New York. 1¾ x 1½.
1255   Stone Fish, looks like a perch, wrought very nicely; No. Carolina. 2½ x 1.
1256   Stone object, looks like the head and body of a snake; from same locality. 2 x ½.
1257   Wrought object, pagoda form; New York. 3 x 1.
1258   Animal-shaped object; Oneida Co., N. Y. 2½ x 1.
1259   Narrow Celt, fine; Meigs Co., Tenn. 2 x ¾.
1260   Narrow elliptical Celt; M. Tenn. 3 x ¾.
1261   Small Tally stone, notched; N. Carolina. 3½ x 1.
1262   Elliptical stone, of red slate or hematite; Lodi, Miss. 3½ x 1.
1263   Small objects, some perforated, one a pipe, others mammals, pendants, etc.; various localities. 16 pcs.
1264   Perforated objects, banner stones, etc.; various localities. 9 pcs.
1265   Hematite Celt, fine and rare; Lodi, Miss. 3½ x 2.
1266   Hematite Plumb bob or small hammer stone; E. Tenn. 1¼ x 1.
1267   Broken Axe of hematite, finely polished; Missouri. 2½ x 1½.
1268   Piece of a hematite Celt, polished; Lincoln Co., Tenn.
1269   Hematite, a large specimen which appears as if patinated or of two separate layers. 4 x 3.
1270   Large piece of Hematite, a fine example. 5 x 2½.
1271   Another fine specimen of the same material. 3½ x 3.
1272   Another piece of Hematite, almost black. 2½ x 1½.
1273   Flat, thin piece of Hematite.
1274   Burnisher or rubbing stone, of quartzite, partly polished, fine; North Carolina. 3 x 2.

1275 Hollow Ball, composed of bog iron ore or limonite, large perforation ; Hot Springs, Ark. 3 in. dia.

1276 Hollow Ball of the same material as No. 1275 ; Hot Spring Co., Ark. 2 in. dia.

1277 Smaller Ball of same material and from same locality as the last. 1¾ in. dia.

1278 Connected Balls, of bog iron ore ; Hot Spring Co., Ark. 2½ x 1½.

1279 Natural formation from the coal mines of Pa. ; two perforations appear at the opposite extremities. 3½ x 1¼.

1280 Velvet Balls of medium size. 6 pcs.

1281 Velvet Balls, smaller than the last. 20 pcs.

SPEAR HEADS, FISH SPEARS AND ARROW POINTS.

1282 Sacrificial Knife, closely resembles the knife used by the Aztec priests in the immolation of human victims sacrificed to the Mexican gods. These knives are mostly of obsidian, very beautiful and very rare. This is of flint and quite as rare as those of obsidian ; W. Pa. 11½ x 3.

1283 Long, narrow Dagger of chert, one of the very finest existing ; Barton, Ala. 11¼ x 2.

1284 Another equally fine and large Dagger of hornstone or chert, probably one of the longest implements of this kind found in America. I have known this dagger for many years, as it was offered to me by the finder ; very rare ; from a large mound 8 miles N. E. of Harrodsburg, Ky. 12¾ x 2.

1285 Another large Dagger of hornstone, point elongated, edge serrated ; from a cache, Danville, Tenn. 8¼x1¾.

1286 Another long Spear head or dagger, of blue hornstone, very fine ; Darke Co., Ohio. 7 x 1¾.

1287 Large Spear head or dagger ; Howard Co., Mo., 6½ x 1½.

1288 Another long Spear head, or dagger ; Missouri. 6½ x 1 .

1289 Large chipped Spear head of broad shield-form ; very fine ; M. Ohio. 6 x 3¼.

1290 Shield-form Spear head; Salt Creek, E. Tenn. 6½ x 2½.

1291 Shield-shape Spear head, of variegated stone, very fine and handsome; Jefferson Co., Ark. 5¾ x 2¾.

1292 Shield-shape Spear head of hornstone, very handsome; Marion Co., Ill. 5 x 2½.

1293 Triangular Spear head, shield form, colors black and white curiously intermingled; a fine and beautiful object. Hot Springs Co., Ark. 5 x 3.

1294 Large shield-shaped Spear head, of handsome light colored feldspar; Williams Co., Ohio. 4½ x 3½.

1295 Spear head of handsome color and finely wrought; Miami Co., Ohio. 4 x 3.

1296 Leaf or shield-shape Spear head; Lincoln Co., Tenn. 4½ x 2¾.

1297 Triangular Spear Head with long stem, fine; Huron Co., Ohio. 5½ x 2¼.

1298 Triangular Spear Head with broad stem, clouded stone; same locality. 5 x 2.

1299 Rotary Spear Head, a choice implement; Shelby Co., Ohio. 4¼ x 2¼.

1300 Long Spear Head or fish spear, fine; Cooper Co., Mo. 6 x 2.

1301 Spear Head deeply serrated, triangular; Huron Co., Ohio. 6 x 2.

1302 Spear Head of chalcedony, leaf-shaped, fine; Shelby Co., Ohio. 5¼ x 2.

1303 Narrow elongated Spear Head, sharp and fine : Tulip, Ark. 6 x 1½.

1304 Handsome Spear Head of chalcedony, translucent, fine; Arkansas. 4½ x 1½.

1305 Elongated Spear Head ; Pulaski Co., Ill. 6 x 1.

1306 Rotary Spear Head, triangular, fine; Barton, Ala. 4½ x 1½.

1307 Triangular Spear Head, ends of the barbs broken; Lincoln Co., Tenn.

1308 Leaf-shaped Spear Head of brownish red color, fine; Pulaski Co., Ill. 5½ x 1¾.

1309 Elliptical Spear Head, edges serrated; Cooper Co., Mo. 4½ x 1½.

1310   Spear Head, barbs deeply notched, fine and rare ; Mo. $4\frac{1}{2}$ x 2.

1311   Spear Head with hollow base, fine ; Franklin Co., Mo. $3\frac{3}{4}$ x 1.

1312   Spear Head, base broad : same locality. $4\frac{1}{2}$ x $1\frac{1}{2}$.

1313   Elliptical Spear Head, rotary and elongated ; Lincoln Co., Tenn. $5\frac{1}{4}$ x $1\frac{1}{2}$.

1314   Narrow pointed Spear Head of black stone, edges serrated ; Ky. 5 x $1\frac{1}{4}$.

1315   Spear Head, edges deeply serrated ; Meade Co., Ky. $4\frac{3}{4}$ x $1\frac{1}{2}$.

1316   Spear Head, elongated and pointed ; Fulton Co., Ill. 4 x $1\frac{1}{2}$.

1317   Spear Head of chert or hornstone, rotary ; Ky. 4 x $1\frac{1}{2}$.

1318   Spear Head of feldspar ; Franklin Co., Mo. $4\frac{1}{4}$ x $1\frac{3}{4}$.

1319   Spear Head, edges notched ; same region. $3\frac{1}{2}$ x $1\frac{1}{2}$.

1320   Spear Head, edges deeply notched, rotary and triangular ; Lincoln Co., Tenn. 3 x $1\frac{3}{4}$.

1321   Spear Head, triangular and rotary ; same location. 3 x 1.

1322   Spear Head, broad triangular, rotary ; Columbus, Ohio. $3\frac{1}{4}$ x $2\frac{1}{4}$.

1323   Spear Head, nearly black, form triangular ; Tenn. $2\frac{1}{2}$ x $1\frac{1}{4}$.

1324   Spear Head, elliptical ; Pulaski Co., Ill. 6 x $1\frac{1}{2}$.

1325   Spear Head, leaf shaped, fine : Lincoln Co., Tenn. $5\frac{1}{2}$ x $1\frac{1}{2}$.

1326   Spear Head, coarsely serrated, a rare form ; Shelby Co., Ohio. $3\frac{1}{2}$ x $1\frac{1}{4}$.

1327   Spear Head with coarse serrations ; Pulaski Co., Ill. $3\frac{1}{2}$ x $1\frac{1}{4}$.

1328   Spear Head with fine serration, of dark grey stone ; Hancock Co., Ky. 3 x $\frac{1}{2}$.

1329   Spear Head, finely serrated ; Cooper Co , Mo. 3 x 1.

1330   Spear Head with fine serration ; Barton, Ala. $2\frac{1}{2}$ x 1.

1331   Spear Head, deeply barbed and rotary, coarse serration, rare form ; Miami Co., Ohio. $2\frac{1}{2}$ x $1\frac{1}{2}$.

1332   Spear Head, serrated. 2 x $1\frac{1}{2}$.

1333   Spear Head, serrated ; Randolph Co., Ill. 2 x 1.

1334   Spear Head of black chert, serrated ; Mahoning Co., Ohio. 3 x 2.

1335   Spear head, serrated and rotary; Breckenridge Co., Ky. 2½ x 1.

1336   Spear head, finely serrated; Pulaski Co., Ill. 3 x 1½.

1337   Spear head, finely serrated and barbed; Tishomingo Co., Miss. 2½ x 1½.

1338   Spear head, barbed and serrated; N. C. 2 x 1.

1339   Spear head or arrow point, rotary and serrated; Miss. 1½ x 1.

1340   Spear head of chalcedony, very fine and handsome; from the west coast of Florida. 2½ x 1½.

1341   Arrow point of clouded chalcedony, a handsome object; Florida. 2 x 1½.

1342   Arrow point of chalcedony, very fine; Florida. 1½ x 1¼.

1343   Arrow point of chalcedony, stained in colors, fine; Florida. 1½ x 1¼.

1344   Arrow point of chalcedony, one barb broken; like the last of variegated colors, very beautiful; Florida. 2 x 1½.

1345   Arrow point of chalcedony, like the last two, of beautiful colors; Florida. 2 x 1½.

1346   Spear head, like several of the foregoing, of fine colors. The rich carmine color is caused by vegetable matter in the salt water in which this was found; Clearwater, Florida. 3 x 2.

1347   Spear head, barbs deeply notched, stone of dark variegated colors; Clearwater, Florida. 3 x 1½.

1348   Triangular Spear head; Florida. 2¼ x 1¼.

1349   Small triangular Spear head; Florida. 2 x 1.

1350   Small Spear head ; Florida. 2 x 1¼.

1351   Small Arrow point; Clearwater, Fla. 1 x ½.

1352   Large Spear head, extremely fine and rare; Denmark. 6 x 1.

1353   Large elliptical or semi-lunar Knife, finely chipped and rare; Denmark. 6½ x 1¾.

1354   Irregular shaped Spear head, of yellow chert; Pulaski Co., Ill. 3 x 2.

1355   Elliptical Spear head, end truncated. 3¼ x 1¼.

1356   Triangular Spear head, thin; Lorraine Co., Ohio. 3 x 2.

1357   Rotary Spear head, fine; Pulaski Co., Ill. 3½ x 1½.

1358   Rotary Spear head, very fine. 3 x 1½.

1359 Long slender Spear head, base hollow; Cooper Co., Mo. 4½ x 1.

1360 Long Spear, slightly curved; same locality. 6 x 1½.

1361 Spear head, curved; Barton, Ala. 4 x 1½.

1362 Elliptical Spear head; Cooper Co., Mo. 5 x 1¼.

1363 Long Spear head; same region. 5½ x 1½.

1364 Semi-elliptical Spear head. 3½ x 2.

1365 Long elliptical Spear head. 4½ x 1.

1366 Long Spear head with base hollowed; Lincoln Co., Tenn. 4 x 1.

1367 Semi-elliptical Spear head, with narrow stem; Ohio. 4½ x 1.

1368 Pointed Spear head, with broad stem; Pulaski Co., Ill. 3¼ x 1.

1369 Spear head, broad, elliptical; Lincoln Co., Tenn. 4x1¼.

1370 Spear head, triangular and pointed; Cooper Co., Mo. 4 x 1¾.

1371 Broad Spear head, one barb broken; Huron Co., Ohio. 3½ x 2.

1372 Spear head of chert; Lincoln Co., Tenn. 2¼ x 1½.

1373 Small Spear head; Gallatin Co., Ill. 2¼ x 1½.

1374 Small Spear head, serrated, with hollow base; Lincoln Co., Tenn. 2¼ x 1¼.

1375 Small triangular Spear head, serrated and rotary; Shelby Co., Ohio. 3 x 1½.

1376 Spear head, smooth with hollow base; North Carolina. 2½ x 1.

1377 Spear head, hollow base; Barton, Ala. 2½ x 1.

1378 Spear head, with hollow barbed base and fine form. 2 x 1.

1379 Jewelry arrow point, fine; Cooper Co., Mo. 1½ x 1.

1380 Arrow point, fine; Lincoln Co., Tenn. 2 x 1¼.

1381 Arrow point, large and fine; Hot Springs Co., Ark. 3 x 1.

1382 Spear head, narrow; Mid. Tenn. 3 x 1.

1383 Spear point, curved and of small size; Lincoln Co., Tenn. 3 x ¾.

1384 Spear point, approaching the triangular; resembles a Scandinavian point; Lincoln Co., Tenn. 3 x ¾.

1385 Spear point, curved; Ala. 2 x 1.

1386   Spear point, slightly curved; Swaine Co., N. C.   2 x 1.

1387   Triangular Arrow point with deep notches; Missouri. 1½ x 1½.

1388   Arrow point, with uncommonly deep serration; Hot Spring Co., Ark.   2 x 1.

1389   Arrow point with hollow base, somewhat drill form; N. Carolina.   3 x 1.

1390   Spear head, sides notched; Meade Co., Ky.   4 x 1.

1391   Spear head, flats chipped longitudinally, of harp form, rare and fine; Lincoln Co., Tenn.   3½ x 1½.

1392   Spear head, sides nearly parallel; Mo.   2 x 1.

1393   Spear head with hollow base; Barton, Ala.   2¼ x 1.

1394   Hollow base Spear head, edges serrated; Pulaski Co., Ill.   3½ x 1¼.

1395   Spear head with hollow base, and stone of variegated colors, fine; Breckenridge Co., Ky.   3½ x 1½.

1396   Spear head, drill shape, edges serrated; Cooper Co., Mo.

1397   Small Spear head; N. Carolina.   2½ x 1½.

1398   Spear head of chert, with hollow base; Lincoln Co., Tenn.   3½ x 1½.

1399   Spear head of drill shape; Randolph Co., Ill.   3 x 1.

1400   Spear head, hollow base, fine.   3 x 1.

1401   Spear head, drill-shape; Missouri.   4 x 1.

1402   Spear head, barbed, hollow base, largely serrated; Chariton Co., Mo.   3 x 1.

1403   Spear head, barbed, with round base; Missouri.   3x1½.

1404   Spear head, serrated, of handsome reddish color; Massac Co., Ill.   3 x 1¼.

1405   Spear head, round smooth base, fine; Ohio.   2¾ x 1¾.

1406   Spear head, round base, red, fine; Lodi, Miss.   2¼ x 1½.

1407   Spear head, nearly triangular, barbed; Lincoln Co., Tenn.   1½ x 1¾.

1408   Spear head, chert, fine; Kentucky.   1¾ x 1¼.

1409   Arrow point, deeply notched; Rabun Co., Ga.   1¼x1¼.

1410   Spear head, narrow, triangular; Lincoln Co., Tenn.   3½ x 2.

1411   Spear head, barbed, triangular; Ky.   3 x 2.

1412   Spear head, rotary, with rounded base; Pulaski Co., Ill.   2¾ x 1½.

1413   Spear head ; Cooper Co., Mo.   3 x 1½.

1414   Spear head of flesh-colored feldspar ; same locality.
3 x 1½.

1415   Spear head of chert; Lincoln Co., Tenn.   3 x 1½.

The following numbers from 1416 to 1446 are neatly arranged on cards
with outlines and localities on the back of each.

1416   Arrow points, some of white and others of milky
quartz, all fine ; from N. C. and S. C.   6 pcs.

1417   Arrow points, one made of a rare variety of milky
quartz ; N. C. and Tenn.   4 pcs.

1418   Arrow points of quartzite, all fine ; Iredell Co., N. C.
4 pcs.

1419   Arrow points, mostly of the kind usually called Oregon points, suitable for jewelry ; different localities.
8 pcs.

1420   Arrow and spear points, made of the rare variety of
quartzite called novaculite, a fine and rare lot ; Ark.
9 pcs.

1421   Arrow points of fine material and beautiful workmanship ; different localities.   12 pcs.

1422   Arrow points, one large and very beautiful, all fine
enough for jewelry ; Franklin and Cooper Cos., Mo.
7 pcs.

1423   Jewelry points, all fine and rare for size and beauty ;
Oregon.   7 pcs.

1424   Jewelry points, fine and handsome ; Oregon.   8 pcs.

1425   Jewelry points made of rare and beautiful novaculite ;
Arkansas.   8 pcs.

1426   Arrow points of white quartzite ; E. Pa.   4 pcs.

1427   Arrow points of white quartz, very fine ; Fairfield Co.,
S. C.   5 pcs.

1428   Jewelry points, six small and one large, the latter
stained and very beautiful ; Ark.   7 pcs.

1429   Fine Arrow points, mostly of white quartzite ; different
localities.   6 pcs.

1430   Arrow points of quartz ; N. Carolina.   4 pcs.

1431   Jewelry points, white and colored, a fine lot ; Georgia
and Ark.   13 pcs.

1432   Arrow points, obsidian, etc., a number minute ; all
from Oregon.   13 pcs.

1433   Jewelry points, obsidian, etc., a fine and rare lot; Oregon. 15 pcs.

1434   Jewelry points, all of obsidian, one has two extra barbs, a rare form, California ; the remainder from Oregon. 15 pcs.

1435   Obsidian Arrow points, a rare lot ; Oregon, etc. 4 pcs.

1436   Drills or borers ; different localities. 7 pcs.

1437   Drills or borers, various materials, all fine ; different localities. 3 pcs.

1438   A similar lot, all fine ; Mo., etc. 3 pcs.

1439   Drills or borers, a fine lot; Ky., etc. 3 pcs.

1440   Drills or perforators, several minute, a fine selection ; different localities. 9 pcs.

1441   Drills, mostly with well formed handles, fine ; different localities. 8 pcs.

1442   Drills or borers, five with large handles, one of extra size ; Georgia, etc. 6 pcs.

1443   Drills or perforators with handles, all fine ; different localities. 6 pcs.

1444   Drills or borers with handles, mostly perfect, all fine ; Missouri, etc. 6 pcs.

1445   Borers with handles; Illinois, etc. 3 pcs.

1446   Rotary Spear head, of red chert, very fine ; S. Ill. 3½ x 1¼.

1447   Fine Spear head, rotary, of chert, serrated, stem broken off; Caledonia, Ill. 4 x 1½.

1448   Rotary Spear head, serrated. S. Ill. 3 x 1.

1449   Shield-shaped Spear head, very fine ; Benton, Miss. 2½ x 1½.

1450   Spear head, bases and barbs rounded, sides parallel ; Barton, Ala. 3 x 1½.

1451   Spear head of chalcedony, suitable for a jewelry point, fine ; Jefferson Co., Ark. 3 x 1¾.

1452   Serrated Spear point, rotary ; Pulaski Co., Ill. 2½ x 1½.

1453   Spear point, harp-shape, base hollowed, fine ; Pulaski Co., Ill. 3 x 1¼.

1454   Spear point, harp shape, base hollowed ; Lincoln Co., Tenn. 2½ x 1.

1455   Spear point, finely harp-shaped ; Barton, Ala. 2½ x 1.

1456   Spear point, elliptical ; S. Illinois. 2½ x 1.

1457 Spear point of dark chert, rotary, fine; Kentucky. 2½ x 1½.

1458 Small arrow point, fine; same region. 1½ x 1.

1459 Small arrow point, suitable for a jewelry point; Dallas Co., Ark. 1¼ x ¾.

1460 Arrow point, serrated, rotary and fine, rare form and material; Barton, Ala. 1¼ x 1.

/ꞓ 1461 Spear head, barbed, fine ; Cooper Co., Mo. 4 x 1¼.

/ ˙ 1462 Rotary Spear head, square base; S. Ill. 3½ x 1.

1463 Spear head, notched ; Pulaski Co., Ill. 4 x 1½.

1464 Rotary Spear head, square base ; S. Ill. 2½ x 1½.

1465 Spear head, barbed and serrated, base smooth ; S. Ill. 2½ x 1¾.

1466 Spear head, sides nearly parallel, serrated; Pulaski Co., Ill. 4 x 1½.

/ꞓ 1467 Triangular Spear head, rotary, white ; Ill. 2½ x 1½.

/ꞓ 1468 Spear head of rough stone, looks like graphite granite ; Yadkin River, N. C. 4 x 2.

/ᴏ1469 Long-pointed Spear head ; Rabun Co., Ga. 2½ x 1¼.

3ᵦ 1470 Barbed Spear head of flesh-colored feldspar, fine ; Barton, Ala. 2¼ x 1½.

/˙ 1471 Long, narrow Spear head, partly black; Knox Co., Tenn. 3 x 1.

1472 Broad Spear head ; Pulaski Co., Ill. 4 x 1½.

ᴛ/ 1473 Small Spear head with hollow base ; S. Ill. 3 x 1.

· ᒿ 1474 Spear head, irregularly notched; S. Ill. 5 x 1½.

ᒪ 1475 Spear head, triangular and clouded ; Huron Co., Ohio. 2½ x 1.

ꞓ 1476 Spear head, bunt shape, short and broad, of feldspar. 1½ x 1½.

- /Ꞙ1477 Shield-shaped Spear head ; Massac Co., Ill. 2½ x 2.

?ᵋ1478 Broad Spear of novaculite, fine and rare ; Montgomery Co., Ark. 3 x 1½.

.· · 1479 Rotary Spear Point, fine ; S. Ill. 3 x 1½.

· 1480 Spear point of reddish feldspar ; Cooper Co., Mo. 3 x 1½.

/ᴏ 1481 Spear head of novaculite, one barb broken ; Arkansas. 2½ x 1½.

/˙ 1482 Long slender Spear head of variegated quartz ; N. C. 3½ x 1.

/ 1483 Triangular Spear head, variegated novaculite ; Ark.
            3 x 1½.

1484 Long Spear head, parti-colored and red ; Ill. 3 x 1½.

' 1485 Broad Spear head, rotary ; Pulaski Co., Ill. 2½ x 1.

'1486 Large broad Spear head, of chert ; Medina, O. 4 x 2.

1487 Handsome Arrow point, suitable for a Jewelry point;
            Ralls Co., Miss. 2 x 1.

1488 Fine Spear head of chert ; S. Ill. 3½ x 1½.

1489 Chert Spear head, good : S. Ill. 4 x 2.

1490 Spear head, white ; Tulip, Ark. 3 x 1.

/ 1491 Rotary Spear head, fine, Cloverport, Ky. 2½ x 1.

1492 Long serrated Spear head, fine ; Cooper Co., Mo. 3½
            x 1.

1493 Broad Spear head ; Huron Co., O. 3 x 1½.

1494 Large shield-shaped Spear head, finely barbed ; Breck-
            enridge Co., Ky. 3 x 2.

1495 Serrated Spear head, barbed. 3 x 1¼.

1496 Spear head ; Decatur, Ala. 3 x 1½.

1497 Shield-shaped Spear head ; Yadkin River, N.C. 2½ x 2.

1498 Spear head, hollow base ; Meade Co., Ky. 3 x 1½.

1499 Broad Spear head of slate, rare ; Knox Co., Tenn. 3
            x 1½.

1500 Narrow Spear head ; Pulaski Co., S. Ill. 3½ x 1.

1501 Large Spear head of chert ; Massac Co., Ill. 6 x 2.

1502 Spear head, coarsely serrated, Montgomery Co., Ark.
            5 x 1½.

1503 Large Spear head ; Pulaski Co., Ill. 5 x 1½.

1504 Spear head, large, described by Mr. Spang as a cutting
            implement ; Massac Co., Ill. 5½ x 1½.

1505 Large elliptical Spear head ; Lorraine Co., O. 6 x 1.

1506 Long-pointed elliptical Spear head, fine ; Cooper Co.,
            Mo. 4½ x 1½.

1507 Large Spear head or knife, found by N. Spang near
            Ocean Spring, Miss. 4 x 3.

1508 Large Drill or borer, broad handle ; Lincoln Co.,
            Tenn. 4 x 2.

1509 Another Drill of the same description ; Meade Co., Ky.
            4 x 1½.

1510 Spear head of citrine or yellow quartz ; N. Carolina.
            4 x 2.

1511 Large broad Spear head of clouded chert; Huron Co., Ohio. 3½ x 2.´
1512 Barbed Spear head of light colored feldspar ; S. Ill. 3½ x 1½.

ARROW POINTS, SPEAR HEADS, KNIVES, ETC.

The following are all numbered and marked in ink and sealing wax, by Mr. Spang. Many of them are very pretty and worthy of a place in any cabinet, and many it will be noticed are of extra quality.

1513 Arrow points and Spear heads, some fine, a good lot. 28 pcs.
1514 Another lot, equal in quality to the last, and like them. 28 pcs.
1515 Another lot of same quality, equally fine. 20 pcs.
1516 Another similar lot. 24 pcs.
1517 Another lot, in every way as good. 20 pcs.
1517a Long, narrow flaked knife of obsidian, *rare ;* Mexico. 4 x 1½.
1517b Flaked Knife of obsidian, long and narrow ; Mexico. 4½ x 1.
1517c Long flaked Knife of obsidian ; Mexico. 4 x 1.
1517d Narrow flaked Knife of obsidian ; Mexico. 4 x 1.
1517e Obsidian flaked Knife, long and narrow ; Mexico. 4½ x ¾.
1517f Long narrow flaked Knife of obsidian ; Mexico. 4½x½.
1518 Sacrificial Knife of obsidian. This knife was used by
   -   the Aztec priests in preparing human victims for sacrifice for immolation before their hideous gods. Their blood was allowed to drain on a square stone which is now shown in the City of Mexico. Large end broken, but a fine and rare implement, sold in the Boban Sale for $21. 10½ x 3½.
1519 Disc-shaped elliptical Knife of chert ; Massac Co., Ill. 5 x 3½.
1520 Another nearly round Knife, also of chert ; Williamson Co., Ill. 3½ x 3.
1521 Sharp chipped Knife of chert, elliptical ; same locality.
1522 Elliptical Knife. sharp ; Pulaski Co., Ill. 3½ x 2½.
1522a Oval Knife of chert ; Massac Co., Ill. 3½ x 2½.
1523 Narrow elliptical Knife, curved ; Caledonia, Ill. 4x1½.

1524   Sharp curved Knife ; same locality.' 5 x 2.
1525   Curved hollow Knife, nicely chipped or flaked ; Piqua,
       O. 4½ x 2.
1526   Particolored flaked Knife, curved, fine ; Olmstead, Ill.
       4 x 2.
⌒ ⌐ 1527   Chipped Knife of dark chert ; Pulaski Co., Ill. 4½x1½.
1528   Curved chipped Knife ; Olmstead, Ill. 3½ x 1½.
1529   Chipped Knife, showing secondary flaking ; Caledonia,
       Ill. 3 x 1½.
1530   Chipped Knife, sharp and curved ; same location.
       4 x 1½.
1531   Weathered flaked Knife ; The Narrows, N. C. 4½ x 1.
1532   Large rude chipped Knife ; Osage Co., Mo. 4 x 2½.
1533   Chipped flake or Knife ; Pulaski Co., Ill. 2½ x 1.
1534   Chipped Flake, variegated colored stone. 3 x 1¼.
1535   Chipped Flake, stained. 2¼ x 1½.
1536   Curved Knife, flake ; Montgomery Co., N. C.
1537   Flaked Knife, curved ; Olmstead, Ill.
1538   Small flaked Knives, some curved. 8 pcs.
1539   A similar lot, fine. 9 pcs.

MISCELLANEOUS.

1540   Plumb bob or sinker, fine ; Massac Co., Ill. 3½ x 2.
1541   Plumb bob ; from Arkansas. 2 x 1½.
1542   Plumb bob of diorite ; Saugus, Mass. 3 x 1.
1543   Box tortoise. Amongst all the objects of prehistoric
       work I have ever seen, this tortoise surpasses all
       that I have met with, and is believed to be the finest
       specimen extant. I do not believe its rival exists.
       4 x 3 x 2.
1544   Spear head of native copper, one of the rarest as it
       is one of the handsomest of copper implements :
       Byron, Wis. 5½ x 1¼.
1545   Metate and roller. This object is of lava, and is used
       by the Mexicans for the purpose of crushing corn
       for frijoles. The object is commonly called in Mex-
       ico a fly crusher, owing to the fact that flies and
       corn are mixed in about equal proportions, prefer-
       ence being usually given to the flies ; metate 5 x 8 ;
       roller 7 x 1½. 2 pcs.

1546 A poisoned Indian Arrow, supposed to be poisoned with venom of snake ; a feathered reed with flint arrow point attached ; Michigan. 28 in. long.

1547 Axe or adze, polished and beautifully wrought. The handle elaborately and artistically carved. The blade resembles jade and is covered and closely wound with sinnet. A fine and rare implement in every respect ; New Zealand. Handle, 24 in., blade, 8 x 3 in.

The following to number 1564 are from the Lake Dwellers in Switzerland, and all from Lake Bienne.

1548 Stone Axe-handle of reindeer horn, very rare. 5 x 2.

1549 Stone Axe with horn handle, axe of green stone. 4x2½.

1550 Stone Axe, handle of reindeer horn. 3 x 1½.

1551 Small stone Axe, handle of reindeer horn, fine. 5½x1½.

1552 Small stone Axe, horn handle. 2½ x 1½.

1553 Another stone Axe with horn handle. 3½ x 1½.

1554 Another of the same description. 4½ x 1½.

1555 Stone Axe or celt, of about the density of obsidian. 1½ x 1.

1556 Stone Bead with perforations, fine and rare. 1½ in. dia.

1557 Needle of reindeer horn, very fine. 6 in. long.

1558 Horn Needle, like the last. 4½ in. long. .

1559 Horn Needle like the others, but smaller. 3 in. long.

1560 Needle of copper, very fine and very rare. 4½ in. long.

1561 Another Needle of copper, rare. 4¾ in. long.

1562 Small Celt of reindeer horn. 2 x ¾.

1563 Bone Celt, like the last. 2 x ⅓.

1564 Another small Celt or knife, of the same material. 2½ x ½.

CELTS, GROOVED AXES, ETC.

1565 Nice granite Celt, edge chipped, partly polished ; Boone Co., Ind. 5½ x 3.

1566 Granite Gouge, partly polished, a scarce implement ; Hamilton Co., Ohio. 5½ x 2½.

1567 Granite Gouge, fine and scarce ; Madison Co., Ind. 5 x 2.

1568   Celt or skinning implement, a scarce object, granite ; Delaware Co., Ind. $4\frac{1}{2}$ x $2\frac{1}{2}$.
1569   Granite Celt ; Marion Co., Ind. $5\frac{1}{2}$ x 2.
1570   Thick Celt ; Hendricks Co., Ind. 5 x 2.
1571   Celt of coarse sandstone, good ; Madison Co., Ind. $5\frac{1}{2}$ x $2\frac{1}{2}$.
1572   Celt of granite, good ; Floyd Co., Ind. 5 x 2.
1573   Broad Celt ; Delaware Co., Ind. 5 x 3.
1574   Celt of black material ; Floyd Co., Ind. 4 x $2\frac{1}{4}$.
1575   Granite Celt ; Marion Co., Ind. $4\frac{1}{2}$ x $2\frac{1}{2}$.
1576   Granite Celt, more than usual size ; same locality. $6\frac{1}{2}$ x 3.
1577   Celt ; also from same region. $4\frac{1}{2}$ x $2\frac{1}{2}$.
1578   Celt, partly polished ; from same locality as the preceding. $3\frac{1}{2}$ x 2.
1579   Celt of coarse granite ; Hendricks Co., Ind. 5 x $2\frac{1}{2}$.
1580   Narrow Celt ; Madison Co., Ind. 4 x $1\frac{1}{2}$.
1581   Narrow thick Celt ; same locality. 5 x $1\frac{1}{2}$.
1582   Thin Celts ; Floyd Co., Ind. 2 pcs.
1583   Large grooved Axe ; Jackson Co., Mo. 7 x $3\frac{1}{2}$.
1584   Large grooved Axe, edge chipped ; Marion Co., Ind. 7 x 5.
1585   Grooved Axe, granite ; Ripley Co., Ind. 5 x 4.
1586   Grooved Axe of granite ; Madison Co., Ind. $5\frac{1}{2}$ x 3.
1587   Long grooved Axe of dark stone ; Floyd Co., Ind. 6 x 3.
1588   Long grooved Axe ; Decatur Co., Ind. $6\frac{1}{2}$ x 3.
1589   Nearly pointed grooved Axe ; Marion Co. Ind. $7\frac{1}{2}$x4.
1590   Grooved Axe ; Jackson Co., Mo. 7.x $4\frac{1}{2}$.
1591   Small grooved Axe ; Floyd Co., Ind. 5 x $2\frac{1}{2}$.
1592   Small broad grooved Axe ; Decatur Co., Ind. $4\frac{1}{2}$ x 3.
1593   Paleolithic Knife, well formed ; Clarksville mound. Floyd Co., Ind. 6 x 3.
1594   Disc shaped, nearly round Knife, paleolithic. $4\frac{1}{2}$ x $3\frac{1}{2}$.
1595   Spade or hoe ; Floyd Co., Ind. 7 x 3.
1596   Paleolithic Knife ; same locality. 5 x $2\frac{1}{2}$.
1597   Paleolithic Knives ; Indiana. 4 pcs.
1598   Rude Knives ; Indiana. 3 pcs.

1599 Knives of the same quality, and from same region. 4
      pcs.
1600 Conical Pestles, one of light the other of dark stone ;
      Indiana. 2 pcs.

BEADS OF BONE, SHELL AND GLASS.

A rare and curious selection from prehistoric mounds and elsewhere.

1602 A necklace of Beads of various material, shell, agate,
      etc. One object strung on this necklace is of red
      slate, a gorget or pendant, sold as numbered, 225
      pcs. All these are rare, many are long cylindrical ;
      Oneida Co., N. Y.
1603 Shell Beads, fine ; a necklace of 109 pcs.
1604 A small Necklace, partly of bone, shell and stone ;
      Georgia. 207 pcs.
1605 Large Beads of shell, called wampum ; dia. about ¾ in.
      42 pcs.
1606 Shell Beads, perforated through their length ; fine and
      large. 8 pcs.
1607 Immense shell Beads, some more than inch thick, large
      perforations ; Lick Creek Mound, E. Tenn. 6 pcs.
1608 Perforated shells of the marginella ; a fine lot. 266
      pcs.
1609 Another marine shell Necklace, each perforated. 92
      pcs.
1610 Shell Beads, mostly of the columella of the conch
      shell. 15 pcs.
1611 Stone Bead, finely polished, rare.
1612 Shell Beads of large size. 5 pcs.
1613 Shell Beads, small. 9 pcs.
1614 Bone, glass and stone Beads. 32 pcs.
1615 Beads of glass and stone. 13 pcs.
1616 Beads of perforated shell. 23 pcs.
1617 Shell Beads, stone, etc. 36 pcs.
1618 Thick shell Beads. 6 pcs.
1619 Beads of stone and bone, several variegated. 5 pcs.
1620 Shell Beads, some with parti-colored coating.
1621 Fine bone Beads, polished ; from a mound in Georgia.
      6 pcs.

1622 Shell Beads of large size, fine. 9 pcs.
1623 Large shell Beads ; from Spang Mound, E. Tenn.
1624 Smaller shell Beads, fine. 33 pcs.
1625 Beads, perforated shells of the marginella. 72 pcs.

The following to 1644 are shown on cards.

1626 Beads, sections of bone and horn, fine ; Peoria, Ill., and Mound, W. Va. 4 pcs.

1627 Bead made of the olivae shell, found with human remains near Peoria, Ill. Another of bone from an Indian grave at Latalle, Ill. ; both fine and rare. 2 pcs.

1628 Needle or awl, made of bone ; Bead made of olivae shell ; another of strombus shell ; from Frazier Mound, E. Tenn. 3 pcs.

1629 Bone Awl and shell beads ; from French Broad and Little Pigeon Rivers, Knoxville, Tenn. 3 pcs.

1630 Bone needle of reindeer horn, fine : Jefferson Co., N. Y. $3\frac{1}{2}$ in. long.

1631 Bone needle or awl ; same locality. $2\frac{1}{2}$ in. long.

1632 Bone implement; mound near Mannsville, N. Y. $3\frac{1}{2}$ in. long.

1633 Bone implement, ploughed up on an old Indian village site, Lincoln Co., Tenn. 2 in. long.

1634 Tooth of a rodent, perhaps a beaver ; small mound, Madison Co., N. Y. $1\frac{1}{2}$ in. long.

1635 Bear's tooth, perforated for necklace ; Carroll Co., Mo. 1 in. long.

1636 A beaver's tooth, found with human bones, implements, etc. : small burial mound, Madison Co., N. Y. $2\frac{1}{2}$ in. long.

1637 Portion of a beaver's tooth and fragment of bone implement ; mound, Madison Co., N. Y. ; each $1\frac{3}{4}$ in. long. 2 pcs.

1638 Portion of a deer horn ; Breckenridge Co., Ky. 2 in. long.

1639 Bone Awl or needle : Madison Co., N. Y. 4 in. long.

1640 Bone implement, perhaps a broken barbed fish spear : small mound, Oneida, N. Y. 3 in. long.

1641 Bone implement, found with human remains, a fine drilled tablet, etc. ; Mound, Madison Co., N. Y. $2\frac{1}{2}$ in. long.

1642 Bear's tooth from the same deposit. 2½ in. long.

1643 Bone implement from the same mound. 3 in. long.

1644 Scales and armor of the alligator; Biloxi, Miss. 12 pcs.

1645 Small univalve shells ; from Decatur, Ala. 3 pcs.

1646 Animal carved from bone, resembles a beaver, neck
perforated : Alaska. 2⅛ x ¾ in.

1647 A duck carved from bone, perforated near the tail ;
Alaska. 1½ in. long.

1648 Bear's tooth perforated ; mound below Galena, Mo.
2⅛ in. long.

1649 Bone implement, probably a model of a hoe, carved
and perforated ; Alaska.

1649a A bear's tooth of large size ; Mound, Clay Co., N. C.
3 in. long.

1650 Shell Hair pin from the columella of the conch shell
or strombus. This hair pin very closely resembles
the fashion of to-day. 7 in. long.

1651 Shell Hairpin, like the last, and equally fine. 6½ in.
long.

1652 Needle of reindeer horn ; Jefferson Co., N. Y. 5 in.
long.

1653 Another Needle of the same material ; same locality.
5 in. long.

1654 Another Needle of reindeer horn ; same locality. 6
in. long.

1655 Implement of reindeer horn, perhaps a pipe stem ; also
from the same region. 4 in. long.

1656 Pointed implement of bone ; Lincoln Co , Tenn. 2
in. long.

1657 Supposed bone implements ; opposite Ocean Grove,
Biloxi, Miss. 2 pcs.

1658 Beaded Pouch, formerly the property of the great
Indian Shawnee chief, Tecumseh, and taken from
his body by Col. Johnson. Presented to Col. U. S.
Monroe by Senator Allen in 1840 at a dinner party
in Ohio, when Allen and Col. Johnson were stump-
ing the State for President William Henry Harrison.
The recent election making Gen. Ben. Harrison
President of the United States, has given renewed
interest to anything relating to Tippecanoe and his
Indian enemy Tecumseh. With the Pouch are flint
and punk. 3 pcs.

1659   Canoe with man seated in it, carved from bone by the native Alaskans. 2 in. long.

1660   Stone Axe with horn handle; from the Lake dwellers of Switzerland, Lake Bienne. $4\frac{1}{2}$ x $1\frac{1}{2}$.

1661   A stone relic described by the finder as " a triangular white stone, with another stone enclosed of the same shape, but of black color "; a very curious and interesting relic; from an Indian grave near Irving, Kansas; each side 3 in. long. $\frac{1}{2}$ in. thick.

1662   A carved object of wood, engraved with twelve faces, nicely done; it appears to be of South Sea Island origin. 4 in. long.

1663   Portion of a buck's antler; from a burial mound, East Pass, Florida. 4 in. long.

1664   Ivory carved Bracelet; from the Solomon Islands. Dia. 3 in., $\frac{1}{4}$ in. thick.

1665   Another ivory carved Bracelet, from the Solomon Islands, perforated, and 28 small beads suspended therefrom. $3\frac{1}{2}$ in. dia.

1666   Portion of a petrified tooth, sawed off; from Ohio river bank, Ohio. 5 x 2.

1667   Shell bracelet, perforated; from the Solomon Islands. 4 in. dia.

1668   Part of a univalve shell, fine; from a shell heap; S. W. Florida. $5\frac{1}{2}$ x $2\frac{1}{2}$.

1669   Agricultural implement of stone, resembles jade, fine; Rideau Lake, Ontario, Can. 6 x $3\frac{1}{2}$.

1670   Nearly globular stone object; Ga. $2\frac{1}{2}$ x $1\frac{1}{2}$.

1671   Small Arrow points, suitable for jewelry; fine; Malvern, Arkansas. 12 pcs.

1672   Jewelry points, similar to the last; Arkansas. 13 pcs.

1673   Another lot of Jewelry points, equal to the last; Mo. 21 pcs.

1674   Fine and rare Jewelry points; Arkansas; each 2 in. long. 2 pcs.

OBJECTS OF POTTERY.

1675   Idol of the ancient Mexicans, the god of the sun, obtained from the wife of the President of Mexico; very fine. 6 x 3.

1676 Human head of pottery, found in a shell heap, Biloxi, Miss. 3½ x 2.

1677 Buffalo head, carved from slate; Wyandotte Co. 2 x 1½.

1678 Human head of pottery, perhaps a jug handle ; Massac Co., Ill. 2½ x 1½.

1679 Handle of a jug of mound pottery, in shape an animal's head ; Macon Co., N. C. 2½ x 1½.

1680 Handle of a pot, a duck's head of mound pottery ; S. Ill. 2 x 2.

1681 Jug or pot handle, of mound pottery ; Biloxi, Miss. 1½ x 1.

1682 Photograph in pottery of an Aztec belle ; near City of Mexico. 2½ x 2.

1683 Animal's head of pottery, a pot handle ; Massac Co., Ill. 2 x 2.

1684 Arm of pottery, perhaps a pot handle : Massac Co., Ill. 3½ x 1.

1685 Photograph of an Aztec swell in pottery ; near Mexico City. 1½ x 1½.

1686 Photograph of an Aztec young lady ; found near Mexico City. 1½ x 1½.

1687 Handle of a pot, with part of the vessel attached, of mound pottery ; Rhea Co., Tenn. 2 x 1½.

1688 Mound pottery jug handles ; different localities, all marked. 4 pcs.

1689 Another lot of jug handles of pottery, like the last. 4 pcs.

1690 Jug handles, etc., of mound pottery. 5 pcs.

1691 Ornamental pottery, one of soapstone ; Mich. 2 large pieces.

1692 Large piece of pottery of soapstone. 6 x 5.

1693 Ornamented fragments of pottery ; from Florida. 7 pcs.

1694 A large red Vase of mound pottery, urn shape ; from a small mound on Evans Island, Jefferson Co., Tenn., capacity about three quarts. 9 x 8.

1695 Mortuary urn of large size ; from the same mound as the preceding, fine ; height 8 in., dia. 7 in.

1696 Large mortuary Urn with large opening ; has a nearly black glaze ; from the same mound, Tenn. Height 7½ in., dia. 7½ in.

1697   Frog-formed Vase or pot, representing a frog in the act of leaping; covered with a black glazing. These figure pieces are all rare ; Arkansas, opposite Memphis. 5 x 3½.

1698   Mortuary Pot or urn, outside covered with leaves indented, glazed, of small size ; Hale Co., Alabama. Height 3½ in., dia. 5 in.

1699   Pot covered with a dark glaze, and surface indented with basket work ; Quallatown, N. C. Height 3 in., dia. 4½ in.

1700   Mortuary Urn or pot, has three handles for suspension over embers or fire, partly glazed ; Miami River, O. Height 3½ in., dia. 5 in.

1701   Mortuary Vase, ornamented with indented leaves, fine ; from an ancient grave, Hot Spring Co., Ark. Height 4½ in., dia. 5 in.

1702   Mortuary Vase taken from a mound near Benton, Arkansas ; surface nearly covered with ornamentation ; has been broken and mended. Height 4½ in., dia. 5 in.

1703   Pot from a mound near Benton, Ark. ; much cracked and mended. Height 7 in., dia. 7 in.

1704   Pot or dish, highly ornamented, mostly in black, perfect. Height 3½ in., dia. 8 in.

1705   Vase or bowl of mound pottery, ornamented with incised lines, mostly black, glazed. 8½ x 6½ x 3 in.

1706   Bottom of a vessel of mound builders' pottery, fine. 2½ in. dia.

1707   An archæological cabinet of black walnut, formerly contained a part of Mr. Spang's collection. It was made to order and was never used but for the Spang collection. Contains 28 drawers of various depths. Size 60 x 38 x 21 in.

1708   Another cabinet, duplicate of the last in size, build and material, in every way equally fine. These two cabinets should go with the collection which is now offered for sale. The pair cost little less than $200.

www.ingramcontent.com/pod-product-compliance
Lightning Source LLC
Chambersburg PA
CBHW032352020726
47499CB00008B/2712